Lilac Island

A Mackinac Island Novella

The Shades of Hope Collection

Linda Hughes

Dedicated to
Joe Martin
my Oklahoma cowboy who loves Mackinac Island

Mackinac: pronounced Mack'-i-naw
We can tell you're a newcomer if you pronounce that "c," which is silent.
It's a French derivative of an Ojibwa Native name for the area.

Published by Kindle Direct Publishing

Cover by MiblArt

✿ Created with Vellum

Chapter 1

2 ⁰²¹

Leah felt as if it was the first time she'd been able to breathe – truly breathe – in months. Casting her face up to the sky, she let the breeze coming off the fresh water whip through her hair, leaving it in playful disarray. Her hands stretched out on the railing, she stood at the bow on the upper deck of the ferry as it churned through Lake Huron on its way to the place that had once been her haven – Mackinac Island.

She wondered if she could handle the memories. Melancholy swept in for a moment yet quickly washed away with knowing that Frank had always said he didn't want her to be morose if he "acquired his toe tag" first. He'd repeatedly said so as they aged. For his unselfishness, she would love him eternally. It allowed her to shift from a sense of loss and self-pity to reflecting upon the blessing of having had such a kind man in her life.

Well, most days, anyway.

They hadn't visited the island too often over the years, seeing that they couldn't afford many vacations, especially when the kids were young. But now she was a sixty-four-year-old widow whose children had gifted her with a little cottage all to herself for the whole summer.

Boldly taking in all that lay ahead, Leah looked out across the deep blue water of the enormous lake. She reveled in the sensation of wild abandon as she scanned the island in the distance; the unmistakable Grand Hotel spread out for what seemed like a mile on her left, its gleaming white porch the longest in the world. Bicycles and horse-drawn carriages, miniatures from this far away, transporting tourists to and fro. Dozens of colorful Victorian-era houses, shops, restaurants, pubs, inns, and B&Bs lining the main street, with more meandering up onto the bluffs. Splotches of lavender dotted the scene, the abundant lilac bushes in lush full bloom.

It's mine. All mine for the whole summer! She took a deep breath of elated anticipation.

Lester sat on the upper deck and watched as the ferry approached the site of the most magnificent and the most wretched summer of his youth. He'd never forgotten and had shunned the island ever since, fearing that stepping foot onto its old-timey streets would bring it all back, his elation over the promise of everlasting joy and then the despair of having that promise disintegrate into ashes before he could take a breath to stop it.

But since his divorce five years earlier, which he'd given himself as a sixtieth birthday present after forty-two years of unhappy marriage, he'd garnered strength. Now he intended to focus on being a solitary guy who didn't need a woman in his life. His uncle had died and left him a small cottage on Mackinac Island, and he was here to stay. Yup. Glorious summer days, blooming flowers, sailboat races, fudge shops, and happy tourists, followed by harsh winters with blizzards, a frozen lake, and isolation. He intended to enjoy every minute of it.

. . .

Cassie sat below deck, fussing with her phone. "Damn. No bars."

She groused to no one in particular, but the woman behind her leaned forward over the seat beside her. "Please keep the foul language to yourself. I have children here."

"Oh, sorry," Cassie mumbled, not meaning it one bit. She looked around. There was a passel of crumbcrushers on this tub, antsy and noisy and annoying.

It didn't help that she'd been in a crappy mood ever since two days earlier when her editor boss had handed her this assignment to write about some island out in the boonies.

"Who on earth wants to go to an island with no cars?" Cassie said.

"You do," the witch quipped, "because you want to keep your job."

"How in blazes will I get around?"

"I have no idea."

It chapped her derriere that she'd been treated with such insolence. Here she was, twenty-six years old and no further in her career than when she'd graduated from college at the top of her class with a Master of Fine Arts degree. Way back then she thought she'd be covering the White House by now. But no-o-o. Despite four years of hard work on a travel magazine, here she was on a ferry on her way to a spit of land in a big lake, having no idea how she'd get around or what she'd write about. Her boss had said, "Make it interesting."

As if that were possible.

She glanced back at the mother who'd scolded her, who now gave her the evil eye. Like a naughty kid, Cassie slunk out of her seat and decided to go above deck to get away from the reminder of her own disapproving mother. She'd been the target of that laser glare way too many times.

. . .

Leah caught herself smiling broadly, her contentment filling her with a sense of empowerment.

"Hey, we're gonna ride horses and see butterflies!" A little boy about four years old rushed up to the rail and announced his upcoming adventure with glee.

"You are? Well, that will be great fun!"

"Sorry," a man said, grabbing the lad around the waist and hoisting him up to carry him away.

Leah glanced back to see the child being seated between his parents, who gently restrained him. She remembered those days when her son could move like lightning and dash away. They had been good days, raising a spirited child. And a few years later, his sister, too.

She looked back at the view ahead. The ferry had come close enough that she could now see the flowers on the lilac bushes. She knew that their alluring scent would welcome her as soon as she alit onto Main Street, the mere thought causing her nostrils to involuntarily flare in delight.

Lester turned his attention away from the woman at the bow and watched a young woman come up to the top deck, struck with how out-of-place she appeared. Tight black pants, long-sleeved black top, fancy black boots. Who dressed like that to visit the island? Ah, he realized, she was a city-slicker who clearly wasn't happy about being here. Slumped in her chair as if trying to become invisible, she perpetually battled with her curly hair as it blew in the wind, frowning and squinting as she looked off at the island in the distance. He could have sworn her frown deepened the closer they got to their destination.

Then the woman at the bow caught his eye again, the one he'd noticed from the beginning. She'd stood in the same spot the whole way, her feet solidly planted like a master sailor, never wavering as the ferry rolled with the undulating waves. He'd watched as an excited little boy scurried up to her, and she exchanged a few words. He hadn't seen her face but could tell she said something nice.

A knot of remorse tugged at his heart, as it often did, at the sight. He'd never had the children he craved, and now it was far too late. He'd concluded that he was destined to be a loner for the remainder of his days. It was dumb fate or some such misfortune.

That woman – he could tell she felt fortunate. He glanced back at the one he'd already labeled as the city slicker, a totally different story.

Cassie surveyed the people around her. It looked like everybody bought their clothes at L.L. Bean or something, as if they were going hiking or bike riding or jogging or, heaven forbid, fishing. Islands were supposed to be sunny places with long sandy beaches and cushy lounge chairs by sparkling swimming pools. She hadn't had time to pack a swimsuit, figuring she'd buy one when she arrived, but these didn't look like languishing-by-the-pool-in-their-bikinis-and-speedos people. She craned her neck to get a good look at the place. Where were the white sand beaches, anyway?

Chapter 2

The captain blew the horn, and Leah could hear the people behind her getting up and rushing to the stairs as the ferry glided into its slip at the dock. She didn't turn around yet. Finally, when the clamoring quelled, she turned and watched as the few passengers left on the upper deck lined up to descend the stairs. There was the couple with the little boy escapee who couldn't wait to ride a horse and see the butterflies, a young woman in black who looked woefully miserable as she stabbed at her hair, and a man about Leah's age, standing straight and proud, as if determined to face the day with fortitude.

The man politely let the others go down first then turned to look at her across the deck. He motioned, gesturing that he'd let her go before him. She shook her head and waved a hand of dismissal. He stared at her for a moment, as if surprised by her response. Something about him made her pause. He'd startled her for some strange reason. He nodded with a gallant touch to his straw fedora, like a movie character from the 1930s. It made her smile.

The man went down and only after she could see that he and everyone else had disembarked did she descend the stairs and walk the plank to the dock. Baggage handlers pushed giant carts of luggage, most tourists having packed way too much as far as Leah was concerned. Some travelers, especially first-timers, didn't grasp what it meant to be on an island where no motorized vehicles were allowed. They didn't realize that many of the inns and B&Bs had bicycle riders carry bags from the dock to their establishments. Some seasoned riders had mastered the art of a dozen bags at a time. Still, it seemed a cruel thing to do to pack a ginormous bag, especially when most of that stuff wouldn't be needed here.

Because she'd be staying for three months, she'd shipped more clothes and her painting supplies ahead. They'd be waiting for her at the cottage, and she itched to start painting the glorious scenes on the island. She loved holding a paint brush in her hand and melding colors on canvas to create a new picture of life. That's what this island meant to her – new life.

She found her roller bag right away and walked onto Main Street. There it was: the soothing aroma of lilacs. Hundreds of the flowery bushes covered the island, and this was the week of the Lilac Festival, Leah's favorite time of the year. Trekking through town and then up a small hill, she arrived in front of the quaint cottage that she would call her own for the summer. It was a lovely little white house surrounded by a white fence with a small yard bursting with flowers. She opened the gate, breathed in the scent of the lilacs, went up the steps to the porch, and found a handwritten note on the door. It had the rental manager's name and phone number, and said, "Mrs. Leah Paganelli, welcome home."

She went inside and made herself at home.

"Mr. Lange!" The livery driver held a sign with Lester's name on it as he called into the crowd flooding out onto Main Street from the dock.

"That's me." Lester flung his bag into the back of the open carriage and hopped up onto the seat with the driver.

"Hello, Mr. Lange. Welcome to Mackinac Island."

"Oh, please, call me Les. And what may I call you?"

"Bob. Plain ol' Bob." The wizened guy lightly flicked the reins. His horse moved forward down Main Street in a practiced gait.

"Well, Bob, you have the address?"

"Yes, sir, I know right where it is. It's a beaut, I tell you. We got her all cleaned up fer ya."

Lester knew the place he'd inherited had been empty for nine months and wondered how much of a "beaut" it could possibly be. He'd find out soon enough.

Cassie was irritated to learn that the B&B her magazine's travel agent had arranged for her didn't have concierge service to transport her bag. She'd have to schlep the thing herself. Thankfully, she'd packed in such a rush it wasn't heavy, and at least it was on wheels.

She turned left on Main Street, walked a few feet, and stopped. Confused, she turned around. The street was full of horse-drawn carriages and people on bicycles, as if she'd slipped into the nineteenth century.

"Excuse me." She confronted a burly man in cargo shorts and a Mackinac Island tee shirt that for some unknown reason said "8.2." He was definitely from this century. "Can you direct me to the Lighthouse Inn?"

"Yo, sorry. I just got here yesterday." He put his hands up as if she'd tried to arrest him and scurried away.

She turned and took a step off the curb but jumped back when a carriage stopped right in front of her. People got off and more people got on. Shocked to her core, she witnessed one of the carriage's horses poop right there on the street.

"Ewww!" She crinkled up her nose as the pungent smell assaulted her. "Aren't those beasts potty trained?"

The carriage rambled on, and a man with a shovel materialized to clear the glop away. Everybody else milled around as nonchalantly as if that sort of thing happened all the time.

9

"The island is full of horses. It's the most natural thing in the world. Think 'old West.'"

Cassie turned to look up and find a cowboy standing beside her. Good looking and knowing it, he wore a teal tee shirt, jeans, and boots. To top it off, a genuine cowboy hat sat on his sandy-haired head. "What?" was all she could come up with, although "Yah-hoo! Look at you!" crossed her mind.

He pulled his sunglasses down on his nose and looked at her over the rim. His eyes were hazel, not that she was staring or anything. "I think you heard me the first time," he said in his Matthew McConaughey voice. Cassie's knees threatened to buckle, but she was proud of herself for standing strong against the onslaught of sensuality. "And the Lighthouse Inn is right down the street, that-away." He pointed in the opposite direction from where she'd been headed. He pushed his sunglasses back into place, cocked his head in a gesture of goodbye, and sauntered on down the sidewalk.

She stretched her neck to watch his backside go "thataway." He went into a bar. At three in the afternoon.

This place wasn't going to be so bad after all.

Chapter 3

"**E**xcuse me, miss. Can I help you? You seem a little lost." Leah stood up from the rocking chair on her porch, shielded her eyes, and stretched sideways to see past the bushes to peer out at the young woman on the sidewalk. Clearly flustered, the woman had been twirling around, cussing, and jabbing at her phone. Her rented bicycle laid on the sidewalk where she'd carelessly dropped it. A branch of lilacs that hung over the fence hit her in the face, and she swatted at it.

Leah recognized her from the ferry the day before, except then she'd worn dreary black clothes. Now she had on white biker shorts, a pale blue tee shirt, a white ball cap, and white sneakers. Tall and slender, she had curly chocolate-brown shoulder-length hair, now pulled back into a puff of a ponytail that stuck out of the hole in the back of her cap. Leah thought she might be of mixed heritage and found her to be uniquely attractive. At least she would be if she didn't look perpetually pissed off.

"Oh. Huh. Um..." The woman stopped, drove a fist into a hip, and glared up at Leah. "Yeah. I guess. Sorry. I didn't know anyone was there."

"Does being lost really require all of that cursing?" Leah had plenty of practice calling out foul language after years of being a high school cafeteria worker. The minute kids got away from their teachers, they thought they could swear like drunk pirates within earshot of the "lunch ladies."

"Um, maybe... not?"

"Probably not." Leah couldn't help but be amused. For some reason, she didn't feel cross with this character.

"I, well, I don't know which way to go to get back into town, and my phone is dead. No GPS." She held up the gadget to emphasize her point.

"Well," Leah said, "can you see down the road there?" She pointed to the street right in front of them.

"Yeah." The woman looked at the street, confused.

"Can you see the water down there?" Leah pointed to where the road ended, a couple of blocks away.

"Yeah."

"On an island, if you head for the water, you'll end up on the road to the town that's on the water."

"Oh, really? Well, hallelujah." The woman caught Leah's tease and sparred like a champ.

Leah chuckled. "Turn left down there. The center of town is a block away.

"Oh." The woman hesitated. "Okay. Thanks." She picked up her bike and, in an unpracticed, gawky move, hauled herself onto the seat.

"Would you like to come up to sit a spell and have a glass of lemonade? It looks like you've been out here for a while, and it's a warm day. I just made a fresh batch." Leah pointed to the side table with her glass and a half-full pitcher, not knowing why she felt compelled to invite this stranger onto her porch.

The young woman stared, then shrugged. Apparently, she didn't know why she'd been invited any more than Leah knew why she'd invited her, but she decided to go with it. She slid off the bike, this time leaning it against the fence, and came through the gate.

"Take a chair while I get another glass." Leah went inside and came back to find her guest in the second rocking chair, looking considerably more relaxed as she smelled the flowers in a vase on the table.

"Here you go." Leah poured a tall glass of lemonade and handed it over. "I'm Leah."

"I'm Cassie. Cassie Evans." Cassie quickly gulped down half of her drink, so Leah topped it off before sitting down. "Thanks. I was parched. Are you a permanent resident of the island? Your cottage is cute." She looked around the porch with its robin-egg-blue beadboard ceiling and peachy pink door.

"No, my children rented it for me for the summer. It's my longest stay ever, so I'm a happy girl. This little place is perfect for me. Aren't the lilacs lovely? They smell so wonderful!"

"There sure are a lot of them."

"Yes, they're in full bloom this time of year. It's the Lilac Festival this week. Is that why
you're here?"

"No. I didn't even know that was going on. I didn't have any prep time. I'd never heard
of this Mackinac Island until a couple of days ago my editor sprung this assignment on me. I write for an online magazine, *Travel Trips and Tips*. Ever heard of it?"

"I can tell you'd never heard of it. You mispronounced 'Mackinac.' The 'c' is silent. It's like Mackinaw."

"Oh. I didn't know."

"No problem." Leah fluttered a hand in dismissal. "That happens a lot. Until you've been here, there's really no way to know. It's a derivation of an Indian word with French spelling, because the French fur traders and missionaries were the first white men here in the 1600s. And to answer your question about your magazine, no, I can't say I've ever heard of it. Where are you from?" Leah figured she knew, but it seemed a polite thing to ask.

"New York City. I'm originally from Delaware, but I went to college in Manhattan and never left."

"I figured the city. I saw you on the ferry yesterday."

"Oh?"

Leah could tell the young woman hadn't noticed her. "Yes, your black outfit gave you away as a city girl."

That elicited a smirk. "I had to buy all new stuff. This isn't my usual style, but it's all I could find." She plucked at her tee shirt. "I hadn't realized I'd be walking and riding a bike so much. Today I went all the way up to the cemeteries." She pointed in the direction she'd come from, where three cemeteries – town, Catholic, and military post – were on the interior of the island. "I didn't think to bring a water bottle, so this hits the spot." She held up her glass in salute.

"Ah, yes, I love those old cemeteries. So much history, and so beautiful and peaceful up there. How long are you staying on the island? I assume you're here by yourself if you're here for work."

Cassie gulped down more lemonade, buying time from what Leah could tell. Her guest carefully wiped her mouth with a napkin before answering. "Yes, I'm here by myself. I'm booked for a week. I'm supposed to be writing something 'interesting' but, so far, I haven't come up with a good angle. It seems like everything has already been written about. I went to the library to search for resources, and there are a ton of them."

"That's true. I read everything I can about the island, and I'd be hard pressed to come up with a new angle. The Native American history, French fur traders, and the British conquering the fort and taking it from America during the War of 1812. That's a battle they don't teach in history books, because we lost." She tittered. "That's great stuff but with lots written about it. There are wonderful coffee table books about the cottages, too."

"Yeah, I get a kick out of them being called 'cottages.' Lots of them are mansions. Those houses up on the bluffs – gorgeous! And the inns and B&Bs are like picture postcards. But there's already a boatload of tourist information out there about that stuff. I don't know what to do."

Leah considered the possibilities. "Have you checked the Island Bookstore? The people who work there are a wealth of information, and they have tons of great resources."

"No, I haven't been there. I'll try it."

"Well, let's see. What else? Lots of people get engaged and married here. But a lot of the love stories have been written about. And there's the classic movie, *Somewhere in Time,* with Christopher Reeve and Jane Seymour. It's a great love story."

Cassie threw a glance her way, frowned, and looked down the street toward the lake. "Truth is," she said, looking back at her hostess, "I'm not much in the mood to write about love. My boyfriend dumped me two months ago. Two years together and he said I'm too 'intense.' Can you imagine?"

Leah knew she didn't dare answer that question.

"Here I am, twenty-six years old, alone, living in a shi...." Cassie stopped, correcting herself. "Living in a crappy apartment because that's all I can afford because I don't make any money in my crappy job."

Leah had no intention of trying to solve this young woman's life problems. She didn't feel sorry for her. But despite the girl's indulgent self-pity, Leah felt a strange sort of tug toward her. She herself had felt "dumped," too, in a way, when Frank died. He hadn't done so on purpose, of course, dying unexpectedly of a heart attack. But she was alone, nonetheless.

Cassie's face brightened. "I did fall in love the minute I got on the island. He's a cowboy. He hated my guts, unfortunately. I saw him go into a bar, and I've gone in there a couple of times, but he hasn't been there. He's probably married with a mistress on the side and has six kids. Just my dumb luck.

"Wow. I have no idea why I'm telling you all of this." The young woman popped out of her web of wretchedness. "You don't even

15

know me. I must be driving you crazy with my drivel. I, well, I'd better go." She finished off her last sip of lemonade and stood up.

Leah smiled. "Cassie, I'm not sure there are any strangers here on the island. There's something magical about this place, a sense of safety maybe, that draws people together. Most of us come here to get away from our daily lives and in doing so, we discover a new way of living. I tell you what, why don't you come back here this evening? You free for supper?"

Cassie shrugged. "Sure. It's not like I've been invited to any grand soirees in those mansions or in the ballroom of the Grand Hotel or anything."

Leah was surprised that Cassie agreed. She'd half expected the girl to make up some obnoxious excuse, like it was her personal mani-pedi night, or she had to watch *The Bachelorette* or some such thing. "Good," she said. "Come at about six. We'll see if we can figure out what you need to write about while we eat."

Cassie nodded and went down the steps and out the gate to retrieve her bike. Before riding away, however, she turned back. "Hey, do you really believe there's something magical about this island?"

Leah grinned. "I sure hope so."

Chapter 4

"What is it about this island, Bob? Here I am thinking of spilling my guts, which I never do." Lester reached into the cooler that sat on the floor between them. He pulled out his second Stroh's of the day – a lot for him – and opened it. He took a big swig.

Bob guffawed. "Whatdaya mean? We jus' discovered we're 'nam brothers, man. A coupla the luckiest S.O.B.s alive because we made it out alive. We mighta been there at different times, but it was the same damned war. That's a brotherhood iffen ever there was one. So, I told ya all about my marriage. Now it's yer turn."

The two men sat on the deck of Lester's cottage, which had delighted Lester when he'd discovered that what he'd inherited truly was indeed a "beaut," as Bob called it. Lester's late uncle had kept the place in excellent repair. Bob had volunteered to come over and go over a few things with Lester, like where the fuse box was located and where to find supplies. Bob and his wife were familiar with the cottage seeing that the late uncle's lawyer had hired them to open it up, assess and perform any necessary repairs, and clean it up before Lester arrived.

Lester nestled into his deck chair and studied his new "brother."

He himself felt like he was still in pretty good shape for a sixty-five-year-old guy, his former lithe but muscular self still lingering on his five-foot-nine-inch frame. Bob, on the other hand, had that skinny-as-a-fence-post look. Six feet four inches tall at least, Lester guessed. Nary a muscle in sight, although he had to be strong enough to handle a horse-drawn carriage. The old saying, he needed to drink mud instead of water so people couldn't see through him, came to mind.

Bob patiently sipped his beer as he waited for a response to his query.

Lester turned his attention to his backyard as he considered how much to tell. A couple of cedar trees blocked the neighbors' cottages, and a white picket fence surrounded the whole property all the way up to the sidewalk out front. Lilac bushes, hydrangeas, and roses – and other flowers that he couldn't name – lined the fence, evidence of his uncle's green thumb. But the dead man had left the back of the fence along the shore clear of vegetation, providing an unobstructed view of Lake Huron with small Round Island and its lighthouse.

The sight calmed Lester and made him consider telling some things he'd never told anyone. What astonished him was that he already felt like he could trust this man beside him, that this man indeed was a brother.

"Your story is a lot less complicated than mine," Lester informed Bob. "You've been married to a feisty Jamaican woman for forty years, you have two nice kids, two grandkids, you've adored your wife since day one, and you claim she even likes you."

"Hard to believe, I know." Bob took the jab with good cheer. "Now, all ya've told me so far is that ya were married fer forty-two years, got a di-vorce five years ago, and here ya are. There must be more to that story."

So Lester told the first part of his sorry tale while Bob sipped slowly on his beer and listened. "As you can see," Lester finally said, "it isn't anything like your life."

Bob remained quiet and, having finished his beer, leaned back in his deck chair with his long, spindly hands behind his head, his bony elbows cocked out on either side. Lester fussed with their now empty bottles, neatly packing them back into the cooler to take into the house.

"Have ya contacted the VA fer benefits?" Bob eventually asked the least personal question possible. It felt like a guy thing to Lester and helped him feel more at ease after revealing one of the most distressing things in his life.

"Yes. I get the usual benefits, of course, and the extra for being affected by Agent Orange."

"Man, I'm sorry that happened to ya. Did people ever bug ya 'bout not havin' kids?"

"Oh, yeah, but my lovely wife liked nothing better than to announce to the world that I had lots of swimmers, but they were all dead." He'd mockingly rolled the word "lovely" around on his tongue. "I think everybody in town knew, right down to the hermit dog catcher."

Bob whistled, low and mournful. "That's bad news, man, havin' her do that on top a' what happened to ya in the first place. I'm one lucky dog, and I know it. Bein' in 'nam a year before you, the same conditions, and nothin' happened to me. Knock wood." He tapped his forehead with his gnarly knuckles. "Happened to a lotta men in my unit, though. All kinds a' health problems. It's so awful how it affected you."

"Truth is, I'm lucky, too," Lester admitted. "My problem has never been life threatening, just heartbreaking. I'd always pictured myself with a family – at least a couple of kids. But my being sterile is nothing compared to what so many of our brothers have gone through. Cancer, heart disease, respiratory disease, disabled children, PTSD, early death. Sterility, like me. Men who had kids before going to Vietnam and couldn't have them when they got home. You name it, and it happens to vets exposed to Agent Orange in much greater numbers than in the rest of the population."

"Did you and yer guys in country used to worry about it when ya saw it being sprayed?" Bob asked. "I mean, we used to watch that bright orange chemical floatin' down from the planes like rain." He waggled his fingers to mimic rainfall. "We'd scratch our heads and wonder how it could be safe fer us if it could kill a whole blasted jungle."

"Yeah, we were worried. But it wasn't like we had any choice but to go about our business."

"Truth is, that whole war never made much sense to me. But I'm still proud to have done my duty and to have served my country."

"Me, too. Even though they drafted us kids right out of our cushy lives that we didn't even know were cushy until they flew us halfway around the world and plopped us into a hell we'd never imagined."

"Ya know, yer lucky in another way, too." Bob pointed at Lester. "How'd ya stay so good lookin' at our age? I'm only a coupla years older, and I look like a withered up old prune compared to you." The man's dark, leathered skin proved his point.

"Awk... Pfft... Dumb luck, I guess." Lester had never been much impressed by what others seemed to consider to be his good looks.

"And how in hell have ya stayed single fer five years since yer divorce? I bet the ol' gals have been all over ya."

"Oh, lordy, I can't have one more friend set me up on a surprise blind date. Don't even try it. You do, and I'll never speak to you again."

"Ya can count on me." Bob nodded emphatically. "But I can't vouch fer my wife Shirley. Once she meets ya, yer a doomed man, what with all her single lady friends."

"I look forward to meeting her, but I'll have to cut her off if she tries that. I'm never getting married again. Oh, I believe in marriage – for other people but not me. Apparently, the right person isn't out there for me."

"Yer marriage was that bad?"

"Hell, yes. God knows how hard I tried, but I could never quite manage it. She's a holy terror." He mulled over his words, realizing he'd never admitted that to another living soul. Well, except to her, and she hadn't cared. "In fact, I only married her before leaving for Vietnam because she said she was pregnant. She'd been my high school girlfriend, and we had one clumsy attempt at making love. But I'd planned the summer here on the island, working for my uncle. When I went home after three months, right away I told her I'd fallen in love with someone here. That's when she sprung it on me that she was pregnant."

"Oh, man, that sucks." Bob shook his head in pity.

"I went to my parents and cried like a baby. My dad told me to 'man up' and my mom said I needed to 'handle' my 'responsibility.' She said I'd ruined that girl's reputation and needed to 'fix' this horrible thing I'd done. I didn't bother telling them that she initiated the whole thing. In fact, I was relieved to be leaving for the summer as a coward's way of breaking up with her. But I had done the deed – sort of. I was the most bungling lover on earth. I think of it as a comedy routine when I remember it now. It was like sophisticated Brigette Bardot trying to seduce a clueless Jerry Lewis."

"Man," Bob said, shaking his head, "my first time was awful, too. I was like a slinky that couldn't control itself."

That made Lester chuckle. "Yeah. But no matter what, in the end, I knew I was in fact responsible for a child that would be coming into this world. I felt like absolute shit. The guilt was unbearable. I was a mess."

Bob chimed up in his new friend's defense. "Ya were jus' a kid, Les. A stupid eighteen-year-old kid. We were all stupid at that age."

Lester nodded. "Well, I was the valedictorian of stupid. I felt I had no choice but to do what my parents told me to do. I married the girl so that our child wouldn't be illegitimate. I buried my love for my Mackinac Island sweetheart, got married, got drafted, and went to war. And I stayed married for forty-two years. I took 'responsibility' to a ridiculous level."

"But I thought ya said ya don't have any kids. What happened to the baby?"

"She had a miscarriage while I was away at war. Or so she said."

21

Bob let out a low whistle. "Whoa, that's a bitch."

"Well, there's more to the story, but I think that's enough for one sitting." Lester stood up and stretched.

Bob got up, too. "Listen, Shirley asked me to invite ya to lunch tomorrow. She's a fabulous cook. Ya free? I mean, with yer busy social schedule and all, I felt it only prudent to ask if ya have the time."

"Ha. Sure."

They discussed the details of where and when, then Bob surprised Lester with an abrupt question. "What was her name – yer Mackinac Island sweetie?"

Lester looked at the rosebushes along the fence, his face brightening in memory. "Rose. Rose O'Grady. I used to call her my sweet Rose on our lilac island."

Chapter 5

1 974

"My sweet Rose on our lilac island." Lester grinned at his pretty girlfriend as she reached up to smell one of the blooms on a fragrant lilac bush.

She plucked the bloom, pushed back one side of her long auburn hair, and stuck the flower behind her ear, its tiny purple blossoms hanging over her silky-smooth cheek. Lester's breath caught in his throat. He'd never seen a creature so alluring.

She picked another one and placed it behind his ear. "There," she mused as she ran a finger across his strong jawline. "My sweet Les on our lilac island."

Lester used his ring finger to brush an errant strand of hair off her forehead. Rose gazed up and him, and the kiss happened as naturally as if it had been preordained by a goddess of love. What followed came naturally as well.

His uncle had given Lester the day off from mowing lawns and had taken the ferry to the mainland for the day. That meant Lester had all day, a first, to spend with his girlfriend. It was an important day, a momentous day, one he knew he'd never forget. It was her last day on the island. Her waitressing job done and her freshman year of college starting in two days, she was anxious, too, to spend every possible moment together. With his uncle gone, Lester had the cottage all to himself. It only made sense to add Rose to it.

They had already professed their love for one another and shared many a stolen kiss, but that kiss by the lilac bush somehow changed everything. They stared into each other's eyes and became trans-formed, no longer two teenagers playing at summertime love. They were two adults who knew what they wanted. And what they wanted was each other.

Like so many working teens, they had come to the island for the summer to make money for college or simply for living. They got away from their parents, some for the first time, and lived in worker dorms or houses. Some, like Lester, stayed with a family member. It was at a party of young workers on the beach in the middle of the night on the north side of the island, away from town, that Lester and Rose first laid eyes on each other. There had been a blazing bonfire and plenty of booze, although neither of them imbibed very much. That night the northern lights had been in a glorious blaze of dancing color, blissfully visible this far north and so far away from city lights. Lester and Rose hadn't met or even seen each other yet and had been looking up at the spectacle in the sky with a crowd of others. But when their eyes came back down to earth and alit on each other, it was as if a brilliant ray from the Aurora Borealis had reached out and electrified them, magically bonding them together.

That bond displayed itself in all its glory that last day she would be on the island when they went back to Lester's uncle's cabin. It had been her first time. Even though she felt an instant of pain, it vanished in the throes of their passion. Lester's need for her, his inability to get too much of her, his joy at her mere touch, obliterated any thought of his first and only other time, blundering and gawkish as it was, with his old girlfriend back home.

When they finally gave in and stopped – not because they wanted to but because the light outside Lester's bedroom window began to fade, and his uncle would be home soon on the evening ferry – they barely said a word. Instead, they opted to hold hands, share a Coke, and look out at the lake. She leaned her head into his chest and cried.

"I'll miss you so much," she professed. "I don't even want to go to college anymore."

"The only reason I want to go to college anymore is to provide a good life for you."

"What?" She backed away and looked at him through adoring eyes.

Slowly, with the grace of a dance master, Lester pulled her back into his body and buried his face in her hair, that luscious mane with its scent of lavender and lilac, a titillating combination of her shampoo and the flower at her ear. He ran his fingers through her long tresses, knowing that he wanted to do this for the rest of his life.

For her part, Rose nuzzled his chest, soaking in the sensation of his fondling.

Collecting all the courage he could muster, he let go of her, stepped back, and took a ring out of his pocket. He held it up for her to see. "Rose, will you marry me?"

She stared at the ring, then stared into his face. He panicked. Maybe he'd gone too far. Maybe it was too early for that question.

But an enormous smile erupted across her face, filling every inch of her lovely features with joy. "Yes! Of course! I will marry you."

He put the antique ring with its diamond chip on her finger, and she gently caressed it, turning it from side to side.

"It's so beautiful," she whispered in awe.

"It was my grandmother's. I told my uncle what I wanted to do, and he gave it to me." She threw her arms around his neck, and they sealed their promise with a luxurious kiss.

Lester had never felt so exhilarated in his life. It was the happiest moment he would know for the next forty-seven years – or perhaps forever.

Chapter 6

2⁰²¹

Leah putzed around her cottage washing dishes, folding laundry, and straightening the pillows on the couch. She floated about to the sound of Hauser's cello and the Piano Guys on Pandora wafting out of her phone. She enjoyed many types of music from this to opera to country to oldies from the '60s and '70s. Ah, the years when she'd been in her prime. Or so it would seem.

But lately she'd felt like this was her prime, soon to be sixty-five years old and learning to settle into a new type of life without a husband. She'd been married since she was eighteen. As traitorous as it felt to think it, being widowed carried with it a kind of freedom she'd never known.

She missed Frank something awful, to be sure. Francesco Paganelli, her vivacious first-generation Italian husband who'd died of a shocking sudden heart attack. Even though there was a nagging emptiness with Frank's absence and a painful yearning to hear his voice one more time, there was also the adventure of discovering that she could stand on her own, that there was a strength in her she'd never known existed. She supposed it was a strength that most people didn't know dwelt within them until they were forced to dig down and find it.

She'd been forced. And she found it.

She went over to her easel and studied the painting she'd been working on, a vase full of every kind and color of flower she could pick from the yard. It was turning into a delightful spray of vitality. She'd spent two hours on it after her surprise visitor, Cassie, left, and she felt supremely satisfied with how it was turning out.

It had been thirty years since she discovered that she had a hidden talent for composition, color combinations, and crafty strokes as an artist. Because of her day job at the school cafeteria, it had always been a hobby. Now, as a retiree, she cherished having time to paint. She picked up a paint brush and considered working on the canvas for a few minutes before Cassie came back for supper.

But after checking the clock on the wall, she saw that it was time to put down the brush and throw on clothes that were warmer than her Bermudas and sleeveless blouse. Evenings on the island could get cool. As she finished changing into jeans and a light sweater, Cassie appeared at the door.

"Perfect timing. Come in, come in."

Cassie had changed clothes, too, now wearing jeans and a tank top under a pink, of all things, hoodie. Her hair billowed at her shoulders. Leah thought her downright fetching this way. She wondered if the girl had any concept of how attractive she was.

"More new clothes?" she asked.

"Yup. It's a new me, I guess. Hey, did you paint this?" On legs that "went up to her neck," as the old saying went, Cassie strode over to the easel and pointed at the canvas. "It's beautiful!"

"Thank you. I love to paint. It soothes my soul. I hope to do a couple of them a week while I'm here."

The younger woman's eyes widened as she looked at Leah with renewed interest. "You have talent, girl!"

"I hope so because I spend an awful lot of time doing it. Okay, let me swipe on some lipstick, and I'll be good to go. I'll only be a second."

In the bathroom, looking at herself in the mirror, Leah realized that she felt pretty, too, like a young – at least a younger than sixty-four-year-old – woman. Oh, she was realistic enough to recognize aging, but she also knew she looked better than she had in years. She'd lost twenty pounds since Frank died. Having become what felt like pudgy but what her husband had called voluptuous, she'd taken care to get the extra pounds off once she retired. And once, sadly, Frank was gone. Not working in a cafeteria and not having a hubby who loved to cook did it. Of course, she knew that if she'd had more will power to begin with, none of that would have mattered. She couldn't blame anyone else for her weight gain. She could, however, give herself credit for taking care of it. Her body felt like herself again.

Lipstick on and hair fluffed, she was ready to go. She felt genuinely happy, she realized. Happy to have what promised to be a new friend, one young enough to be her granddaughter. She had a granddaughter who was a few years younger than Cassie, a college student who'd earned a scholarship to study in Europe for the summer. She and Leah had always been close, and Leah missed her. It would feel good to spend time schmoozing with a young woman again.

In fact, Leah decided she was simply happy to be alive. It was with that attitude that she drifted out into the night, open to whatever the world might bring her way.

"That's him! That's him, that's him, that's him. Don't look!" Cassie struggled to keep from squealing.

Leah couldn't help but look. "Where?"

"No, no! Don't look. It's too obvious."

"You're looking. Why can't I?" Leah teased.

"Okay, he turned his back to us. Now you can look." Cassie pointed to a man at the bar of the restaurant.

Leah rubbernecked. There were a lot of people at the bar but the tall one with the broad-shouldered back and wearing a cowboy hat had to be him.

"The cowboy you fell in love with the minute you hit the island? The one who hates your guts?"

"Yeah. That's him. It's the first time I've laid eyes on him since then."

"Why don't you go talk to him? If he already hates you, what damage can it do? Maybe you'll change his mind."

"Think so?"

"Sure. Go for it." Leah pulled Cassie's wine glass out of the way so the girl wouldn't topple it in her excitement.

Cassie started to slide out of their booth but froze.

Leah turned in time to see the cowboy greet an attractive woman who walked up to him. Spreading his arms out wide, he gifted her with a great big bear hug.

"Well, damn. I mean darn." Even in the throes of her disappointment, Cassie corrected her swearing, which Leah appreciated. "Apparently, he has a blasted girlfriend."

"Maybe not. It could be his sister."

"Oh, really? You are so-o-o optimistic. Maybe even naive."

They both stared as the cowboy and the blasted interloper sidled out of the place.

"I want to go to the nearest fudge shop and get a ginormous brick of dark chocolate fudge for dessert," Cassie moaned. "You in?"

"Always."

"Which do you prefer: Ryba's, Murdick's, Joann's?" Cassie counted them off on her fingers.

"Ah, you've already partaken of the fudge. Did you know the shop workers call the tourists 'fudgies'?"

"So I hear. I'm proud to be one."

They finished off their wine and paid the bill. As they headed out, Leah had an intriguing incident of her own. Jostling amongst patrons coming and going at the door, she bumped into a man who was going in. They passed one another, and she looked back to find that it was the man who'd been on the ferry, the guy her age who'd worn a straw fedora. Now, sans hat, she could see that he had thick silver hair. And he was handsome as all get-out. She actually felt her heart flutter, something she hadn't experienced in... how long? Forever. He glanced her way, and their eyes met, and Leah could have sworn she knew him. But the crowd moved on, the moment passed, and she figured she was simply imagining things.

Besides, she'd been widowed for less than a year. It didn't seem right to be attracted to another man already. Or was it? But at her age? Was she merely a silly old woman trying to recapture her youth with such a ridiculous notion?

She didn't know the answers to any of those questions.

Chapter 7

Lester looked back at the comely woman he'd accidentally bumped into at the door of the restaurant, and a pang of attraction struck him. How odd, he thought, to have such a strong reaction to a stranger. He'd immediately recognized her as the woman on the ferry who stood like a feisty sailor at the bow. Strong. Steady. And appealing.

Yes, he admitted to himself, he might be a shallow old coot for not minding that a woman was attractive. Especially that kind of attractive with her natural good looks, gray steaks in her ebullient hair, and laugh lines around her bright eyes.

But beauty wasn't all that mattered to him, so maybe he had more depth than he gave himself credit for. He chalked up a checkmark for good character in his mind.

After all, his ex-wife was and always had been gorgeous. Everybody they knew thought so. As the years went by, she had every plastic surgery procedure known to humankind, or at least ever fathomed by Lester. He'd been the one who'd felt obligated to work his butt off to pay for it, seeing that she'd never found it "convenient" – her word, not his – to get a job.

All that attention to beauty, and it had never mattered to him.

33

He'd much rather have been with someone who felt good in her own skin, like the woman from the ferry seemed to feel.

He thought of these things as he ate alone at a small corner table in the restaurant, unable to get the sight of that woman out of his mind – and the feel of her nearness out of his body. That brief encounter at the door rattled him mightily. It made him wonder if he was ready to relinquish his vow to be a loner. Maybe – just maybe – he was finally ready to start dating again if it could be someone as interesting as her.

She'd been with a young woman who looked something like one on the ferry, but with a totally different vibe. So this one must be somebody different. He wondered if this young woman was the ferry woman's granddaughter. Although, they didn't look alike. The older woman was only about five feet three inches tall, and the younger one was probably five ten. But stranger things happened in families.

Families. He'd lay odds that she had a nice one. That meant there might be a nice husband out there, too. Maybe he wasn't with her because she was on a girl trip with her granddaughter, who she met up with on the island. Or maybe not. Maybe there was no husband. Suddenly, he became driven to find out.

By the time his cherry pie came for dessert, he was strategizing how to find that woman. And, more to the point, what to do if her found her.

Leah and Cassie strolled along the shore on the west side of town, soaking up a warm summer evening. It hadn't chilled down at all, with a balmy mist rolling in off the lake, giving everything a mystical glow. Muted lights from boats skidded over the water in the distance, and from this vantage point, they had a full view of the Mackinac Bridge, its purple nightlights in honor of lilac time pulsing with the flow of the haze. The women found a bench and sat down facing the lake.

"It really does look magical out here tonight." Cassie took in the full expanse of the bridge that connected the lower and upper peninsulas of Michigan.

"Yes, it does," Leah agreed as she opened her fudge box and cut a piece with the plastic knife provided. She downed the dark chocolate chunk in one bite.

Cassie worked on hers, and they ate in silence for a while. It's hard to talk with a mouth full of heaven, Leah thought.

Finally, she wrapped up what was left of her fudge and closed the box. "I might explode if I eat any more." She set the box aside.

Cassie ate a few more bites and put hers up, too. "I might explode, too, but it would be worth it. I never knew something so simple could taste so good."

"That was such a nice dinner. And this was the perfect dessert. Cassie, have you thought anymore about what you want to write about for your article?"

"I sort of have. Something about people coming here to heal – emotionally. You gave me the idea. You said people come here to get away from their daily lives and find a new way of living in the process. 'Getting away from' what? And what do they find? You, for example. I don't want to pry into your life if you don't feel like talking about it, but over dinner, you mentioned that you're a widow. Why did you come here?"

Leah didn't know what to say.

Cassie threw up a palm to signal stop. "Don't answer that. For now, I'm only using it as an example. I bet there are a lot of people here because they need to heal from some kind of pain. Even me, and I didn't even want to come. I feel different, though. I can't put my finger on it yet, but something is happening to me. I might be turning into – God forbid – a little bit of a nice person. I actually forgot to take my phone with me when I went to the fort this afternoon. Can you imagine?"

Leah chuckled. "No, I can't. The ghosts in that old place probably loved you. They must be sick to death of people with their cell phones in hand."

"Hey, that would mean at least somebody loves me. I really enjoyed that place. The story about the British taking it in the War of 1812 and the American soldiers hightailing it out of there, and some of their wives got left behind. And there's a rumor that while the British were there for two years, some of the wives got to liking them better than their husbands. So when the Americans got the island and the fort back, some of those wives were none too pleased to see their men again."

Leah nodded. "I know, I know. Those poor women."

"Yeah, they would've been able to tell some good stories. I think I'll see what I can conjure up and use the healing angle.

The mist turned to heavy fog as they walked home, and they became cloaked in a world of mysterious wonder. They passed by Cassie's B&B first, leaving Leah to go a couple of blocks alone to her cottage. Walking down those old streets at night in the fog gave her an exhilarating sense of otherworldliness. The world had more dimensions than were obvious.

It struck her that she did, too, and Cassie might as well.

Chapter 8

"Have you ever tried finding her?" Shirley wanted to know. Bob threw up his hands. "Honey, I'd say something about us havin' jus' started our meal, but I know it won't do any good."

"Oh, he can talk and eat at the same time. Can't you, Les?" Bob's wife Shirley patted the table beside their guest's spoon.

Les had liked Shirley the moment he walked into their tiny apartment. As broad as Bob was thin, with big hips and a generous bosom, she wore a dress patterned with bright flowers and a loud apron that clashed with each other. It tickled Lester that she didn't try to hide her build and apparently wore whatever she liked. Her black hair was short with a few beaded cornrows, the rest doing as it pleased. And her Jamaican accent was charming. Her directness was actually a relief to him. No pussyfooting around. Les could feel himself slipping into uncharted territory again, the telling of his story.

"Yes, I can talk while I'm eating," he said, answering her question. "But I promise not to talk with my mouth full."

"So have you tried to find her?" Shirley repeated her question. Bob had filled in his wife before Les arrived, so she was ready to get down and dirty.

Les swallowed his bite of salad. "I did, actually." He forked a slice of tomato and ate it. "While I was in Vietnam, my wife sent me a letter saying she'd lost the baby. From that moment on, I knew what I'd do as soon as I got home. The minute I stepped back into our apartment, I told her I wanted a divorce. Then I got into the car I hadn't driven in a year and went straight to Rose's hometown. I didn't know if she was still there, but it's a small town, and I figured I could find someone who would tell me where she'd gone. I'll never forget it. I parked on the main street, got out of my car, glanced in a café window, and there she was. My heart stopped right in my chest. I couldn't believe it. I'd found her like that." He snapped his fingers.

Lester finished the final bites of his salad. Shirley remained quiet for as long as she could manage. "And?" she burst out.

"I started for the door when I saw a man lean across the table and stroke her cheek. I'd been so focused on her I hadn't noticed him before. He was handsome. The opposite of me. Dark hair. Dark eyes. Exotic, I suppose women would say. A Latin lover type." Lester looked away from his companions, lost in memory. "The way she looked at him. It was obvious she adored him. She took his hand from her cheek and kissed it."

Shirley let out a long breath, at a loss for words. Bob seemed surprised by her silence, and he was glad to remain mum, too.

After a heavy pause, Lester came back to them. "I got back in my car and went home to my wife. I never looked for Rose again."

"But... but, she could be divorced by now or widowed or who knows what. You should try again." Shirley was adamant as she got up from the table to clear the salad plates and stack them in the sink. She went to the stove, put on oven mitts, and pulled out a pan of lasagna. The smell drifted across the table, and Lester's stomach growled with desire. She served enormous helpings, which pleased him, because he wanted a lot of this stuff.

Once she sat back down, she threw Lester an impatient look. "Well? Are you going to look for her again or not?"

"I don't think I can." Lester took a bite of the cheesiest lasagna he'd ever seen. "Holy moly, Shirley, this is the best lasagna I've ever had in my life! You're a brilliant cook."

"I know," Bob agreed. "This is one of my favorites." He ate with exuberance.

"Rose," Shirley reeled Lester back into her topic at hand. "Why can't you try to find her now?"

"Well, for one thing, I'm not the same man she knew. I'd be a stranger to her. I came home from war wounded. Not physically, but in my mind. I wasn't that carefree teenaged boy anymore who thought life held nothing but goodness. But more than that, when I saw that she was happy with someone else, two things happened." He heartily ate another bite then stopped, holding his fork midair. He looked from Shirley to Bob, considering how far he wanted to go with this conversation. "I've never admitted this to anyone else in my life, but Bob, you might be able to relate."

Bob nodded. "Okay. Hit me."

"I was jealous. There I'd been, living in hell, killing guys my age, not even knowing why. All the while, she'd been happy. With another man. As much as I loved her, I hated her for that. I was jealous not only of him but of her, too, of her happiness."

"But didn't ya tell me ya never contacted her after ya left the island? I mean, there she was thinkin' she was engaged, and ya disappeared." Bob had a good point in Rose's favor. "Don't ya think she was probably heartbroken? Who can blame her fer findin' love elsewhere?"

"Of course. On a logical level, my brain knew that. But my heart was sick with jealously."

"Oh, that poor girl." Shirley patted Lester's hand. "And poor you. What a tragic love story, all the way around."

"Ya know," Bob said, "I do understand. I remember feelin' something like that, too. Comin' home and my friends and family members had jus' been goin' on with their lives. They had no way of knowin' what it was really like over there. And I wouldn't have wanted them to know. But I didn't fit in anymore."

"Yes. That's it."

They ate in near silence for a while, the only conversation revolving around passing the garlic bread and complimenting Shirley on her cooking. Eventually, Lester and Bob talked about the Lilac Festival and how busy Bob had been driving the carriage with all the tourists in town.

They finished their meal, and Lester wiped his mouth with his napkin, neatly folded it, and put it on the table. Shirley caught him off guard with another question.

"What was the second thing?" She didn't miss anything. "You said two things happened."

While she pried, Bob picked up their empty plates and took them to the kitchen sink. He returned with three mugs hanging from his long fingers on one hand and a coffee pot in the other. He poured three cups and passed them around as Lester mulled over the inquisition.

Lester pushed back his chair and rested his clasped hands at his waist. "A part of me, the part that still loved her, was overwhelmed with happiness for her. She looked content. Safe. I was so very glad for that. She was as beautiful as ever. She probably still believed in goodness. Being with me would have tainted her world. I didn't want to do that to her. I was glad she was happy. I know, it doesn't make much sense. I hated her for being happy but still loved her deeply, which made me glad she was happy. I have no way of explaining that away. It's just the way it was. It was a horrendous battle that wrestled with itself all the way down to my soul."

Shirley stared at him for a moment, her eyes watering with sadness. In a soft, comforting voice she said, "But you wouldn't taint her world now, would you? I mean, you're a good person who might be able to share a good life with someone you love. You've come to grips with that war, haven't you? I know Bob has." She took her husband's hand in hers, and they smiled at one another in the kind of mutual understanding that comes with years of living and loving together.

"Oh, yes." Lester's voice became gentler, too. "I think I did that years ago. We have to in order to survive. But now I would be a stranger interrupting her life. And she's probably still married to that exotic Latin lover dude, whoever the lucky bastard is." He slowly sipped his coffee, as did his hosts.

"Well, I know what we need," Shirley announced, setting down her mug. "Cake!"

She went to the fridge and pulled out a fat red velvet cake with plump cream cheese frosting, leaving Lester to wonder how on God's green earth Bob could possibly be so skinny.

Chapter 9

Leah and Cassie stood on the sidewalk in front of Marquette Park on Main Street, waiting for their carriage to arrive. The park was teaming with people of all ages enjoying the exquisite weather. With the temperature in the seventies, and with pillows of fluffy white clouds floating by in the vivid blue sky, it was a perfect day for frolicking around outdoors. The marina across the street bustled with activity as yachts and sailboats came and went.

Cassie looked up at the statue of a man in a long robe in the center of the park grounds. "Who's that?"

Leah took in the statue she'd seen a few times before. "Father Jacques Marquette, a Jesuit missionary who came here in the 1600s to try to convert the native tribes to Christianity."

"Did he succeed?"

"I suppose. It got him a park named after him and a statue."

"Well, that's more than I'll ever get."

"When you toured the fort, did they tell you this used to be the army's vegetable garden?" Leah gestured to indicate the park.

"No, I missed that." Cassie looked back at the imposing white stucco fort on the bluff behind the park, its long, white-walled, diagonal walkway leading to the entrance its most identifiable feature.

"I think I see our carriage." Leah had turned away from the park and peered down the street. When she called for the reservation, she'd been told the carriage would be a four-seater, which included the driver who was named Bob. It was an open buggy, and seeing that most had overhead coverage, she figured that one way down the street would be theirs.

Both women stretched to get a better view. The behemoth brown horse strode their way, pulling the carriage with the driver and another man in the front seat. It stopped in front of St. Anne's church, a beautiful white building with stained glass windows and a tall, white spire. The non-driver hopped out, and the men waved a quick goodbye to each other.

Something about that scene niggled at Leah. She took a few steps to get a better look. But a gaggle of bicycle riders whizzed by, and she lost site of the man who got off. By the time the cyclists moved on, that man had disappeared. The carriage closed the distance between it and them and pulled to a stop in front of them.

"Hello, ladies. Are you Leah and Cassie?"

"That we are," Leah said as she climbed up into the backseat.

"Yup. Cassie here." The younger woman hopped in with much more dexterity than Leah ever remembered having. "And you're Bob. Right?"

"Yes, I am, miss. At yer service. What would ya ladies like to see today?"

It turned into a grand adventure, with a tour of the East and West Bluffs with their picturesque Victorian era "cottages." They went to the Governor's Mansion, and Bob patiently waited while the women went on a short tour inside. The view of Lake Huron from the veranda was stunning. Leah took photos on her phone and hankered to paint that view. Then they went by the Grand Hotel, and she photographed more grand vistas to memorialize on canvas.

On their way back into town, Cassie leaned toward their driver and said, "Bob, how long have you been driving a carriage on the island?"

"Oh, jus' since I retired five years ago from my job at the factory in De-troit. My wife and I used to love to visit up here, and this job is a great way fer us to stay fer the summer."

"So you drive but don't own the horse and carriage?"

"Correct. I work fer the owner. He has lots a' carriages. But Molly and I are good ol' friends. She's been my horse every year."

"You must meet all kinds of people in this job. Who has been the most interesting?"

"Cassie, you sound like a journalist," Leah chided.

Bob reminisced about some of his more interesting riders but concluded with, "Of course, present comp-ny surpasses them all."

His riders chortled at that.

"Would ya mind if I make a quick stop right here at the stables? I have a question fer the vet who has one a' our horses."

They agreed that was fine, and Bob pulled onto a side street and up to a barn. He jumped down and hustled inside. The women could hear talking, and then Bob came out – with the cowboy at his side.

Leah thought she'd have to hold up Cassie lest the poor girl faint dead away. She watched as the two young adults spied each other. Cassie froze, but the cowboy had no problem striding right up to the carriage and taking a gander at Cassie's gams in her short shorts. It was a long take.

Bob read the awkward exchange and interrupted it. "Leah, Cassie, this is Russ, the island veter-narian in the summertime. Russ, these fine ladies are here fer a visit."

Leah wanted to laugh out loud. She restrained herself. "Nice to meet you, Russ. I believe you and Cassie have met but have never been introduced."

"That's right. Cassie..." He put his hands up on either side of the narrow door opening to the back seat of the carriage and leaned in an inch. "... I assume you found your way to the Lighthouse Inn."

Cassie recoiled away from him, burrowing into Leah. "Yes. Yes, I did. Thank you." Her voice was ice. She nervously uncrossed and recrossed her legs like a flamingo who didn't know what to do with them.

Determined to thaw the girl out, Leah pressed on. "So, Russ, you're here in the summer. Where do you live in the wintertime?"

"I'm from Oklahoma. I have a veterinary practice there with my brother and..."

The pretty woman from the bar, the one he'd given a bear hug, suddenly appeared out of the barn. "Russ! Where's the bridle for Samson?"

Leah felt Cassie freeze up again, this time into a block with the superpower to commit serious harm. She might explode into the air with a "pow" of a fist at any moment, aimed at that woman.

"I hung it on the peg by the door." Russ threw the answer over his shoulder.

The woman went back inside.

Russ looked directly at Cassie, even though Leah had asked the question. "As I was saying, I have a practice in Oklahoma with my brother and my sister." He jabbed a thumb at the barn. "That's my sister."

Now Leah really wanted to let loose with a howl. She elbowed Cassie in an "I told you so" gesture.

Cassie immediately melted. "Your sister? She's a vet, too?"

"Yessiree. Our brother handles the practice back home while Miranda and I are up here."

The moments of silence that followed while Cassie and Russ stared at each other caused the two older adults to look at each other. Bob shrugged. Leah shook her head. Wise enough to read what was happening here, they didn't interrupt. It probably wouldn't matter if they tried.

Finally realizing they were gawking, the young couple let the spell break.

"So, Bob." Russ pried his eyes off Cassie. "As I said, tell your boss his mare will be fine by tomorrow. He can pick her up then."

For her part, Cassie brimmed with delight all the way home.

Leah enjoyed this development immensely, although a stab of long-lost sorrow came with it. It brought back memories of the time so long ago when she'd first fallen in love. A time when she thought she'd never be hurt. A time when she thought anything was possible. Well, she reckoned, Cassie was older than she'd been, and this wasn't the girl's first rodeo. Hopefully, Cassie would at least enjoy herself and, at the most, find true love.

Ah, if there was such a thing.

Chapter 10

C assie looked down at her feet, twisting one leg sideways and then the other, and twirling the skirt of her short summer dress to get a good look. Never in a million years would she have guessed she'd someday wear cowgirl boots. They were quite unique, she decided, with the brown leather tooled in a turquoise and red Western design. But totally not her usual style.

Not that she objected to boots per se – real boots like her closetful of them at home in New York City. When she'd lived with her boyfriend and had a few spare bucks, she always bought boots. Three pairs of ankle boots, one pair with punky silver rivets; three pairs of knee boots, one pair with fringe at the knee, which made her feel particularly feisty; and two pairs of practical snow boots. Plus, there was the pair of ankle boots she'd worn to the island and hadn't touched since arriving.

"What do you think? Do they feel okay?" Russ' sister Miranda had insisted on loaning the cowgirl boots to Cassie when she learned they wore the same size, saying that Cassie's sandals would never do for what Russ had planned for the evening. Cassie still had no idea what that might be.

"They feel great. Thank you. It's very kind of you to give up your boots to a virtual stranger."

Miranda's face slowly drew out in a sly smile. "Oh, no, never mind. I brought eight pairs with me this summer."

"Hey, that's how many pairs I have at home."

"I'd bet my bonnet yours and mine look nothing alike."

"You'd be right. Mine are all black."

"Black? Don't you like color?"

"Sure, I guess. But I've become used to wearing black."

"Everywhere? All the time?"

"No, of course not. Sometimes I wear gray. Or light blue. Geez, I guess that is pretty boring, isn't it?"

Miranda nodded and bit her lower lip until breaking out in laughter. Cassie joined in, realizing she liked this woman she'd wanted to tackle and drag away by the hair on the night she'd seen Russ give her a hug in the bar.

"Miranda, where is Russ taking me tonight? He won't tell me."

"Uh uh. Not telling. It's a big secret. But, actually, everybody else on the island knows about it." Her eyes glistened with mischief. "After all, it's a tradition during Lilac Festival time. Come on, let's go show off your new look."

They left the bedroom and went into the living room of the family cottage. It turned out the veterinarians' mother was from Michigan, and this summer home had been in her family for generations. Russ, Miranda, and their three siblings had grown up spending summers here.

Cassie had been charmed upon entering the place. Russ had picked her up in the late afternoon, and they'd walked up the bluff to the cottage. She felt flattered that he wanted to show it to her. The cottage – unpretentious compared to many on the island – sat hidden away off a dirt path that meandered off Pottawatome Road, behind the grand cottages on the East Bluff. Not visible from the road, she'd been delighted to walk up the porch steps and turn around to discover that it had a spectacular view of Lake Huron, with Round

Island and its lighthouse in the distance, and Bois Blanc Island, the larger island off to the left.

It was without a doubt a porch for lingering and enjoying the scenery, but when Russ led her inside, she instantly fell in love with the whole house. Cozy and relaxed, it felt like a place for letting go of life's worries. With vintage Persian rugs and beautifully crafted antique furniture, it somehow didn't feel stuffy. She realized it smelled like lilacs, noticing the large vase of them on the oakwood dining room table. This house had seen many years of family gatherings, and it showed.

When she and Miranda went back into the living room, they found Russ looking out the beveled glass windows, taking in the view. He turned toward them, took one look at Cassie, and clapped. "There! Now you're ready."

"Ready for what?"

"Come on. You'll see." He grabbed her hand and down the lane they went, headed for town.

She heard it before she could see it. Country music, with somebody loudly crooning about a "Boot Scoot Boogie," could be heard blocks away. When they reached Market Street, a hundred street dancers dressed in Western fare were line dancing with raucous gaiety. Russ pulled her into the fray, and Cassie did her best to try to keep up. Always a step behind, shaking her head, she caught herself laughing out loud. To her utter amazement, she was having a good time.

By the time they ate tacos at a picnic table by the shore, she'd become comfortable with Russ, who turned out to be as unpretentious as his house. Salt of the earth, grounded, and downright sexy to boot. There was only one problem.

He interrupted her thoughts. "Are you thinking about what an unlikely duo we are? I ask because I know I am."

"Actually, yes. I mean, our lives are so different."

"Right. Your life is in New York City."

"And yours is here and in Oklahoma. I confess, I still can't hear the name of your state without thinking 'Ooooh-klahoma, where the wind comes sweepin' down the plain....'" She broke into song, pumping her arms from side to side to mimic the hoedown dance moves from the famous musical. "I saw the play on Broadway. Great music."

He chuckled. "You could come visit us sometime. See it for real."

"I could? I mean, sure, I could, couldn't I?"

They stared at one another for a minute, and Russ reached over the table to take her hand. Cassie easily settled into the feel of his touch.

"How much longer are you here?"

"Four days. I have to get going on my article for work that I told you about. I haven't done much on it yet. Mostly, I've visited the library and done research."

"What're you going to write about?"

She looked out at the lake that reflected the signs of dusk. "I read about the Native Americans who used to come here before the French fur traders and missionaries arrived. You must already know that story: tribes from all over gathered here each summer to trade and visit and matchmake. Thousands of people came, and hundreds of teepees and lodges and canoes lined the shore. They considered the island to be sacred. Well, I've come to think of it as sacred, too. It was Leah who first made me think of it, of how people come here to experience new ways of living so they can heal from the stress and problems back home."

Russ considered that, eventually saying, "I like it. I like it a lot. I look forward to reading it. I've never thought of it exactly as sacred to me, but now that you say it, it fits. It's sacred to me because it harbors so many of the animals that I love, and I get to do the work I love, and it takes me back to a time that feels like it's where I belong. And it's beautiful."

Cassie smiled. "That helps me with my story. Don't worry, I won't write about you, but I bet that happens for a lot of people."

"How about you? What's happened for you here?"

She wanted to shout, "I'm falling in love with a cowboy! How ridiculous!" Instead, she said, "I'm learning that I don't have to live the way I've been living if I don't want to."

"Do you want to?"

"I have yet to figure that out." Cassie looked down at the cowgirl boots on her feet. These feelings of being drawn to Russ were crazy. Nothing could possibly ever work out between them.

They drifted into the darkening night, not knowing where they were going.

Chapter 11

A cool breeze invigorated Leah as she peddled her bike heading north up the west side of the island. Officially, this road was M-185 but was called Main Street in town and Lake Shore Drive otherwise. It went all the way around the island, an easy 8.2-mile ride that followed the flat shoreline. It was the only state highway in the country that didn't allow motorized vehicles, which was the case for the entire island. For that, cyclists could enjoy their rides without constantly looking over their shoulders to make sure they wouldn't be struck down by a lumbering hunk of metal.

Leah rode on without concern. To her left, the sun inched its way toward the water on the horizon, telling her that her timing would be perfect for reaching the shore below Sunset Rock, supposedly the best spot on the island for watching the sun go down. She would take photos as prompts for painting.

Over the years, she and Frank had enjoyed a few sunsets at that spot, and she knew that his absence would make this an emotional evening. For that reason, she'd wanted to come alone and hadn't invited Cassie. That girl was probably busy with Russ, the cowboy veterinarian, anyway. The thought made Leah happy.

She passed Devil's Kitchen, a covey of small sea caves, but kept going. This stretch of road was desolate, especially this time of day. Most of the island was a state park, its woods and shoreline untouchable for habitation. Woodlands lined the road on her right, and the water's edge meandered along her left, the ebb and flow of the waves a soothing backdrop for her journey.

She thought about how in 1875, the island had been designated the second national park after Yellowstone. But when Fort Mackinac was decommissioned, the island was given back to the state and became Michigan's first state park in 1895. Leah loved the history of the place.

Frank had loved it, too, the thought bringing on a stab of sadness. Sometimes she ached for his warm presence beside her, for the little things that were big things – his hand softly placed on the small of her back as they entered a doorway, always knowing that he literally had her back, and his quiet companionship during moments like this.

Her sorrow dissipated when a few other cyclists, much more ambitious than she, tooled past her, waving as they went. They turned a corner and disappeared, again leaving her alone on the road, feeling spooked and brave at the same time. It was impossible to settle on one feeling, so she let any and all of them ramble around inside her, colliding with one another to leave her emotions a jumble.

More cyclists came up behind her as they reached their destination. It was time to watch the sun go down. The riders who had passed her had stopped there, too, so a small crowd gathered to watch as the sun sizzled into the lake, leaving a prism of brilliant pink and orange and yellow rays stretching out toward them across the water, as if reaching out and pleading with them to respect the majesty of the earth. At least, that was what it felt like to Leah. The photos she captured were stunning, including a few of the colorfully lighted Mackinac Bridge far away.

The others bid her goodbye and rode on. Once again, she was alone. But was Frank there with her? It often felt as if he watched over her, protecting her from unhappiness or harm. She knew that a psychiatrist would probably say that was simply a leftover sense of security that she'd become accustomed to after so many years with him by her side. She knew she had to get used to the reality that he was gone but wondered if he'd ever really leave her soul. There was good and bad in that, something she hated to admit to herself.

On her bike again, she ventured into the dusk and stopped at a beach where she and Frank had made cairns. There were at least fifty of the stacked pebbles along the shore, most a foot or so high, some especially creative. Builders had to find the right stones that would balance, one on top of the other. She loved the tradition of building something so delicate that would be swept away in the weather, which meant that the builder had to return to do it again. Therefore, one could never entirely leave the island.

She photographed a few cairns in the dim light, then decided to break with tradition and make a pattern on a large flat rock rather than a piled-up cairn. The rocks and pebbles on the island beaches were bewitching, with striated colors and fossilized patterns, so she used her flashlight to find ones she thought the most prophetic. Carefully, she spread them out on the rock to make a big heart. Satisfied with her work, she sat down on the edge of the big rock and peered out at the water, which became more mysterious by the moment as the earth turned on its axis and enveloped her in darkness. Stars appeared in the sky, especially bright on this moonless night.

It was then that Leah started to cry, a sobbing from so deep within her she never would have been able to say from where it came. "Damn you, Frank," she groaned. "Damn you for leaving me alone like this."

She'd long ago admitted to herself that for most of their marriage she'd resented her husband, the man who appeared to be so perfect in the eyes of others. Her children adored their father, and for that reason, she would never utter a word to anyone about how irresponsible he'd been. Outgoing, vivacious, good-natured, helpful, protective – yes. He never missed one of the kid's games. He sat on the town council and the vestry of their church. He was there when anyone needed a helping hand. But Frank Paganelli never made a living. Not a real one, at least. Coddled by his Italian parents, who Leah adored even though they'd spoiled their son, he worked in their shoe store and did anything he pleased, from leaving in the middle of the day to go bowling to taking a day off for no reason other than he didn't "feel like" going in. Consequently, he'd been at a total loss when that family store went belly-up. The business had never been particularly successful, so he made a meager salary to begin with. So there he was in his thirties, unemployed, with a family to feed, and no prospects. Friends who owned businesses hired him from time to time, but it never worked out. Frank simply wasn't accustomed to real work.

Living with Francesco "Frank" Paganelli had been like living with an adorable, loveable, untrained puppy.

Thus, Leah had made a thirty-two-year career of working in the school cafeteria, where she could get health insurance for her family and set aside a small retirement fund. Thankfully, she'd liked her job, but it only paid enough to barely keep them going. She'd needed help, which came in brief spurts from her husband as temporary jobs came and went.

Frank often apologized that he didn't contribute more and promised to do better. She gave up believing that after ten years. He settled into repairing lawn mowers in their garage. At least he was doing something, she often thought, and he wasn't robbing banks. Although sometimes she wished he would rob a bank. It would have made her life a lot easier.

She hated herself for thoughts like that. Of course she didn't want her husband to have broken the law. What she wanted was relief from the full burden of their financial responsibility falling on her for most of their married life.

So she cried, out there in the black night, all by herself, sitting on a rock on a remote shore on Mackinac Island. For the thousandth time, she asked herself if she'd truly loved Frank. The answer was always the same: yes. Despite it all, she couldn't imagine a better father to their children or a better companion to her in every way that didn't include money.

Somehow, catharsis set in, and she felt better. As she dried her eyes one final time, more cyclists came by, night riders like herself. Their bicycle headlights on, all she could see were beams in the dark until they reached her side. It would have been a scene from a horror film had this not been Mackinac Island. Inviting her to join them, she hopped on her bike, turned on the headlight, and lit out for what she knew would be a spectacular display in the night sky up ahead.

Chapter 12

Lester had done this plenty of times that one summer he'd been here so many years ago. At age eighteen, however, riding a bicycle around the island in the dark of night seemed like a great adventure, especially because it usually involved a gang of kids his age. All by himself at age sixty-five, however, he became rather freaked out, seeing ghosts lingering in the treetops and filtering up from the rocks on the shore. Bah! He shook his head. He didn't even believe in ghosts. He cast the ridiculous superstition aside and kept peddling.

His destination was one he'd been thinking about ever since arriving on the island. He didn't know if it would bring back fond memories or encase him in the doldrums. He was about to find out.

The bike left to him by his uncle didn't have a headlight, so he'd jimmied up a flashlight on the front fender. It wasn't doing a lot of good, its faint illumination hitting the road only two feet in front of him. He didn't remember this road being so blasted dark at night, like riding through an unlit cave.

The Mackinac Bridge sat so far off in the distance, its lights didn't help him at all. But still, he managed to see the part of the shore strewn with cairns. He stopped, suddenly remembering the tradition.

Intrigued, he grabbed his flashlight and went over to look. Some were feats of engineering. Some were childlike. And one wasn't a cairn at all. There on a large flat rock was a big heart made with pretty pebbles. It inspired him to pick up half a dozen stones and stack them up inside the heart. A cairn enwrapped in love. He liked the idea and nodded approval, imagining that the creator of the heart would like it, too.

Sitting down on the edge of the big rock, he stared out into the black Great Lake. Lately, he'd been thinking about needing to let go of his old life. His thoughts wandered back to that night five years ago when he'd finally told his wife he wanted a divorce, once and for all. All those years of marriage, forty-two years of angst for him in deciding to pull the plug, and she'd laughed. Merely laughed.

"I wondered if you'd ever get around to that," she'd said. Then she nonchalantly told him that she'd had half a dozen affairs over the years. He'd always thought that despite all their difficulties and differences, loyalty to one another was the one stable thing they'd shared. He'd been shocked to learn otherwise. He doubted his sanity, wondering if he'd been living in a blithering delusion.

But she didn't stop there. She told him that there never had been a pregnancy when they got married. She'd never wanted children. The fact that he came home from war with "dead swimmers" was a bonus for her.

She'd lied so he would marry her, thinking he was going to college to be a big-time engineer, the career he'd said he wanted. When he was drafted and sent to Vietnam, she'd been disappointed but still thought a cushy future lay ahead. She despised him when he came home from war and decided to skip college to become a carpenter.

When he asked why she'd stayed with him all those years, especially since he'd never made the financial fortune she craved, she said he'd been steady and "convenient." That word again, one of her favorites. Once he started remodeling historic homes and public buildings, and acquired a reputation for his craftsmanship, she liked being married to someone people in the community admired. And the money was better, although nothing to brag about, she said.

On that night, their last night in the same house, Lester realized it was the first time his wife had ever been honest with him. At least he had to give her that.

He thought about his work, how he loved working with his hands. Restoring historic buildings soothed his soul. He loved those old places, the surprises behind walls and under floors, the weathered tight-grained wood, his visions of the lives lived in those antique spaces. No, he'd never become wealthy, but he'd been happy in his work and supposed it was one reason he'd been willing to put aside his unhappiness in his marriage for so long. That career had indeed been steady, allowing him to put away a comfortable sum for retirement, even after dividing assets in the divorce.

Still, as many times as he'd analyzed his life, too often he came out of it feeling like a fool for letting himself live a lie for most of his adult life, believing he had a faithful wife. But while sitting there on a rock in the black of night on Mackinac Island, he decided to let it go. He wasn't a fool but rather an incurable romantic. That wasn't a bad thing.

He affixed the flashlight back onto the front of his bike, hopped on, and kept going. Then what he'd been aiming for happened at the turn past Chimney Rock; he could see the edges of the magical Aurora Borealis, the northern lights caused by the solar wind interacting with the earth's atmosphere. By the time he reached the British Landing, the historical spot where the British had come in to take over the island during the War of 1812, the pulsating lights in the sky were magnificent. When he reached Point Aux Pins, the place of the pines at the northernmost tip of the island, the spectacle was on grand display.

Lester's jaw dropped in a silent "wow" as he peddled backwards to stop his old-fashioned bike. Standing with the bike still between his legs, he simply stared in wonder.

After a few minutes, he set down his bike and joined the small group silently sitting on boulders along the shore. Another group, who had apparently arrived earlier and had already been there for a while, was heading out, riding away from him. He barely glanced their way, his attention so drawn to the dancing neon lights in the sky, until something made him look at their backs as they disappeared like ghosts vaporizing into the night.

What was it that drew his attention to them? He didn't know. He thought of the woman he'd come to think of as the "ferry woman." He'd looked for her ever since bumping into her at the restaurant. She hadn't been back there, from what he could tell from regular checking, and his stints in the park and sitting on the marina wall watching the crowd had been fruitless, too. Ah, he decided, silly to think he'd find her here. After all, riding a bike in the middle of the night was quite bonkers.

As for his memories of being here when he was eighteen years old, he found that they were not moribund after all but came upon him in a sweet wave of warmth. It was here that he'd met Rose O'Grady, the girl he'd fallen in love with. It was here that he'd felt the promise of a happy future with her. It was here that he'd enjoyed the innocence of youth.

Gone now for sure. But the feeling of having loved so purely imbued the incurable romantic in him with dreams for his future. Was it truly possible to be having these thoughts, especially after vowing never to love again? Yes, he was surprised to find that he was having thoughts of falling in love again. Perhaps all was not lost, even at his age. The hopeful young man he'd once been came out of hiding and showed himself. Shockingly, he still resided in the old man's body.

Lester got back on his bike and went on his way.

Chapter 13

"Leah, it was the most exciting thing I've done in ages. No! Ever. The most exciting thing I've ever done!" Cassie paced back and forth on the porch while Leah painted. Leah had brought her easel outside to enjoy the glorious weather while she worked on a canvas of the view from the Governor's Mansion. Cassie had shown up a minute earlier.

Leah glanced up at the younger woman. "You've never been on a horse before?"

"No, of course not. I mean, where do people get horses anyway? That is, besides here. Oklahoma, I guess, because Russ sure does ride well. He rodeos."

"Really? That's cool. What does he do in the rodeo?"

"Um, I don't know. Whatever they do in rodeos. Ride horses and stuff. They lasso cows with ropes." She mimicked lassoing. "I've seen that in movies."

Leah chuckled. "Next time you see him, ask about it. Make him think you're supremely interested in learning all about it. It'll make him happy."

"Good idea."

"So let me get this straight: last night you two went out line dancing, ate tacos, had a great time, and somehow he managed to get you on a horse early this morning?"

"Yes. And I despise getting up early. But this was so much fun. I was terrified at first, but he got me a gentle old mare and we stayed in a thing..." She twirled her hand in a circle.

"A ring?"

"Yeah, that's it. I felt like a warrior queen, way up there looking down at everyone. I love it. And I love Betsy, my horse. I think she likes me, too. She whinnied at me when we were done. I called it snorting but Russ said it's 'whinnying'."

"Well, this is quite a development." Leah put down her paint brush and wiped her hands on her painter's apron.

"By the way, your painting is beautiful. You are really good at this."

"Thanks. How about a drink?" The older woman ran a forearm across her forehead to swipe back her wayward hair. "Lemonade? Tea?"

"Your lemonade is the best. Here, let me help." Cassie followed her inside, and within minutes, they were back out in their rocking chairs, savoring their drinks.

"How was your evening after you danced and ate?"

"Great. I mean, we both talked a lot and laughed a lot. I thought we had fun. Then when he walked me home, I was disappointed because he was perfectly proper. He kissed me on the forehead at my door. I figured that was the big brush-off if ever there was one. But I decided that was okay because there's so obviously no future for us together. I mean, we live in different worlds. So I promised myself I wouldn't fall for him. Then when he showed up this morning asking me to come learn to ride, I totally forgot my resolution to not like him. And I realized that by kissing my forehead, he was maybe being a gentleman. I'm not sure I've ever met one before. Do you think there's such a thing?"

Leah thought back. Her bike ride around the island the night before had revived memories from long ago. "Yes. I knew one such young man. I was smitten the moment I saw him. He was a perfect gentleman, too, kissing my hand the first time he took me home. But it got better after that." She chuckled and felt girlish again at the memory.

"Do tell!"

"No, I can't."

"Come on. I need to know. Aren't we besties by now who share these things?"

The two women were laughing when Bob rolled up in his carriage. "Hello, ladies!"

"Bob!" Leah waved as she and Cassie ambled out to the gate.

"Hey, there," Cassie chimed in.

"I have an invitation fer ya from me and my lovely wife Shirley. We're havin' a barbeque this very evenin', with a group a' friends and neighbors. I'm tellin' ya, ya do not want to miss Shirley's pulled pork barbeque or Jamaican jerk chicken. Um-um good!"

"I'm in." Leah nodded, her mouth already watering at the thought.

"Me, too," Cassie said.

"Seeing that our place is so small, and our apartment complex doesn't have any yard to speak of, Russ and Miranda have agreed to let us use that great big yard by their barn. It's only a few blocks from here. Remember?" He pointed in the direction of the barn where he'd stopped when he'd given them a carriage tour when they'd met Russ.

"Sure. What time?" Leah asked.

"Six o'clock. Russ said he'd like to escort both a' ya ladies, and he'll walk over to pick ya up. Is that okay?"

Leah looked over to watch Cassie beam. "Yes," Leah said, "I do believe that's fine. What can we bring?"

"Oh, lordy, ya've never seen how much Shirley cooks. Nothin' needed."

"A bottle of wine?"

"Why, yes, that would be nice. See ya then." He gently flicked the reins, and Molly carried him away.

As they walked back to the porch, Leah said, "Well, my girl, it looks like we both have a date tonight with that handsome young cowboy."

Cassie shrugged. "I'm happy to share, because I sure as hell don't know what to do with him."

Chapter 14

Cassie watched in total confusion as Leah led the man away. After all, Leah and Russ and she had arrived at the barbeque party only minutes earlier. Savory smells permeated the air. Twenty people milled around, drinking from plastic cups and bottles of beer. They waved at Bob, who worked a grill, and Russ introduced them to Shirley. Leah handed over the wine bottle she'd brought to Shirley, who handed it off to another guy, who took it to the beverage table and went to work opening it up.

Then, out of nowhere, a man appeared at their side, straw fedora on his head. Cassie remembered seeing him on the ferry. Actually, she remembered the hat. She was pretty sure Russ introduced him as Lester Lange, but Leah had looked so stricken she'd been paying attention to her friend's reaction. Consequently, she wasn't sure she caught the man's name right.

Leah leered at the man and said, "Lester, I'm Leah Paganelli. Come with me, please." Then the woman abruptly walked away. The man, that Lester, followed her like a smitten teenaged zombie. They disappeared around the side of the barn.

Cassie and Russ, totally befuddled, watched them go.

Shirley thrust her fists onto her hips and quipped, "Well, butter my biscuit. If I'd known it was gonna be that easy to get those two together, we wouldn't have needed to bother with all this whole shabang." She swept an arm around the crowd.

"What in blazes was that all about?" Bob walked up, waving the grilling tongs in his hand. He'd seen it, too. "Shirley, you are the best matchmaker ever, my love." He gave her a playful sideways hug and bussed her temple.

"I guess so. I have far more talent than I realized." She shook her head in wonder, still staring at the spot where the pair had disappeared.

"You mean this whole party is a setup to get those two together?" Russ pointed toward the corner of the barn.

Bob nodded vigorously. "Uh huh. As soon as I told my bride here that I'd taken two nice ladies fer a carriage ride, and one a' them was a widow about our age, Lester was doomed, no matter how much he objected to bein' set up."

Shirley shrugged. "My work here is done. Let's eat, everybody!"

Totally flummoxed, Lester had no idea what was going on. But seeing that he'd spent the last three days trying to find this woman, he wasn't about to ignore the miraculous gift of her appearance out of nowhere, like an angel descended from the heavens.

She led him to the far side of the barn where they had privacy. He followed without question, feeling like a fawning teenager. The feeling didn't bother him.

She stopped beside a lilac bush and turned to him. He stood stock still, almost afraid to breathe, taking in every inch of her beguiling face. Shaking his head, he apologized. "Pardon me for staring. It's just that you remind me so much of someone I used to know, a long time ago. Your eyes..."

"Forty-seven years ago, to be exact."

"What?" Lester couldn't fathom what he'd heard.

She plucked a lilac from the bush and twirled it in her fingers.

"Lester, I am Leah Rose O'Grady Paganelli. You knew me as Rose O'Grady. Remember?"

"Rose?" It came out as a mere whisper, his voice having abandoned him. His mind raced back to the past. His Rose! They'd stood like this by a lilac bush. She'd put blossoms like this in their hair. She would reach up at any second and do it again, touching his ear as she placed the lilac there!

She tossed the lilac to the ground. "Yes. It's me. How are you, Lester?"

His inner voice screamed, "I'm in love with you, that's how I am!" His actual voice managed, "I'm okay. How about you?"

"I'm good...."

Chapter 15

An hour later the one-time lovers arrived at Leah's gate after having walked around town. The truth was, she'd had conflicting impulses to both kiss him and spit on him the moment she realized who he was. Those jumbled up emotions still clashed inside her head. After all, once upon a time she'd been madly in love with him, and then he'd so callously shattered that love. However, it had been so long.... She didn't know how to feel about him now.

Their conversation floated on the surface, as if they were afraid of what they might find out if they dove in too deep. Neither of them mentioned the summer of 1974. She told him she was widowed; she had two children, three grandchildren, and one great-grandchild; she'd enjoyed her job at a school; and now she was retired and loved to paint. He told her he was divorced; he had no children; he loved his job restoring historic buildings; he'd moved to the island; and, although he was supposed to be retired, he was happy to already have some restoration jobs lined up here.

They spoke of how they'd noticed each other on the ferry, having no idea they had a long-lost connection. And they recalled bumping into each other at the restaurant.

But beyond that, they were like two teenagers on a first date. Awkward.

"We totally forgot about the barbeque, didn't we?" She eventually realized, laughing.

"Yeah, I'll apologize to Bob and Shirley tomorrow."

"Lester, it's been a surprise to see you again." She opened the gate and walked through. "I'm glad you've been okay all these years." She thought that maybe she meant it, at least a little.

"Yeah, well, do you mind if I steal a few more minutes of your time to tell you something about that? I promise it won't be too gruesome. But I really need to apologize."

She considered that for a moment. Did she honestly want to know why he'd abandoned her all those years ago? Yes, of course. She'd always pretended that she didn't, but she did. "I guess so. Let's sit on the porch."

Once settled, his hat off his head and placed on the side table, Lester leaned forward, rested his elbows on his knees, and faced her. "Rose.... May I call you Rose?"

"I suppose. I was always Rose growing up but, once I got married, I decided to use my first name." She didn't add that once he dumped her, it hurt too much to hear the name Rose.

"Rose, I've been trying to figure out how to say this all night. I still don't know what's the best way, but here it is: I need to apologize to you. In fact, I should flail myself and grovel in the dirt and beg your forgiveness. I want you to know that I did fall in love with you that summer in 1974. I was head over heels. Ready to marry you if you'd have me. When I gave you my grandmother's ring... Do you remember that?"

"Of course. I still have it. I always saved it because I knew it had been a family heirloom and thought maybe someday, if I ever ran into you again, I'd give it back. I'll send it..."

"No, that's not why I brought it up. I want you to know that when I gave you that ring, I sincerely meant my proposal. But I'd had a girlfriend back home before I came here. When I got back home, she told me she was pregnant. I was devastated. We'd only had sex one time. My parents pushed me to marry her. I know that's no excuse. I was old enough to make my own decision, but I didn't. I was a total idiot juvenile wuss. I married her. I didn't see any other way. I simply wasn't smart enough to figure out another option, like staying single and sharing custody. I was bringing a child into the world. I couldn't abandon it, no matter what. My feelings didn't matter anymore."

"You married her because you felt responsible?" Leah did her best to imagine how traumatic that must have been for him and reeled with the irony of it all.

"Yes."

"Hmmm. That was noble. Especially for an 'idiot juvenile wuss.' Maybe you're not giving yourself enough credit for making the right decision." Her mind spun with awareness, so many missing puzzle pieces crashing into place.

"Maybe so, but I didn't have to leave you in the lurch. I didn't have the guts to go to you or even call you to tell you what had happened. I've never forgiven myself for that."

She couldn't suppress a smirk. "Well, that was rather wussy."

"Yeah, it was pathetic, wasn't it? I might have built up the courage to call you in time, but I got drafted and was in Vietnam before I knew what had happened to me."

"I wondered if you got drafted."

"While I was there, my wife wrote to tell me she'd had a miscarriage. So when I came home, I told her I wanted a divorce. I went to Dexter, Rose. I went to your hometown to try to find you."

"What?" Her gasp came from deep within. She'd always thought he'd abandoned her. Discovering that he'd been so close was news that truly stunned her. If only she'd known.

"Yes, and I found you."

"What? I never knew you were there."

"No, because I saw you through a restaurant window with a dark-haired man, who I assume was your husband. You were so tender with each other. My heart broke at the same time I was glad you were happy. I was glad you weren't a wreck like me. I left and went back to my wife."

"Oh, Lester, I had no earthly idea. And here I thought you'd simply cast your silly summertime love affair out the window and forgotten all about me."

He looked into her eyes. "No. Never. But my life became more complicated after that. It turned out I was sterile because of Agent Orange and couldn't have any more kids. I was devastated. Eventually, though, I had to face the reality that I was never going to have the family I'd always pictured in my head. I had to throw that picture away and get on with my life."

Leah felt her eyes mist. It was a touching story, one that tore at her heart because of the futility of it all. "You wanted children?"

"Yes. I would have loved having a family. I don't think I ever let myself admit, though, that it wouldn't have been a good idea to have one with my wife. I never stopped thinking of you."

She didn't know what to say. He'd always thought of her? All the while, she'd been busy raising kids and supporting a family. She hadn't spent much time thinking of anything or anyone else.

Or had she? When lying in bed at night, right before falling asleep, there had often been that lingering feeling there was something missing in her life, something she could never quite grasp. Something she'd only experienced that summer she'd fallen in love with the teenaged boy who had become this man. Sometimes she dreamt about being on Mackinac Island, lying on a blanket on the sweet summer grass with the sumptuous smell of lilacs filling her with a sense of sheer contentment. Then she'd wake up, and the longing would return.

"Can you ever forgive me, Rose?"

Leah got up and spread her hands out on the railing. Lester followed and noticed that she'd taken the same stance at the bow of the ferry. One that would keep her steady.

"Lester, I admit that you destroyed me. I felt abandoned and stupid. I thought I'd totally misread our situation. I had been so in love with you, I could hardly think. But then when I got home and never heard from you again, real life settled in. I had no choice but to face reality. Then Frank came along, and I moved on with my life." Of course, it hadn't been that simple, but she wasn't ready to talk about that yet. She sighed. "As the years have gone by, I've realized that something might have happened to you that was beyond your control. My teenaged angst gave way long ago. I'm so sorry for what happened to you. How awful."

"Oh, I'm not asking for pity from anybody, least of all you. I was one lucky soldier that I came home at all. Believe me, I'm grateful to be alive. And I love my work. I have good friends. I feel fortunate in many ways. I haven't had it all, but I've had enough to have a good life."

That warmed Leah's heart. She took the twinge of pity she'd felt for him and cast it away, which helped her jumbled emotions calm down. She almost felt dizzy with the revelation of it all. "The answer is yes. I can forgive you."

"Thank you, Rose. That means the world to me."

She nodded acceptance of his gratitude. "Are you free to come over for lunch tomorrow?"

"Of course."

"Come at noon, and I'll cook us something. I'm a great cook." She turned toward the steps, indicating that their evening together had come to an end.

Lester let loose with a smile and took a step toward her. "Rose, may I, well, may I..." He stretched out his arms in invitation.

She accepted and slid into his embrace, nestling her head into his broad chest. Backing away, she said, "Good night, Lester. I'll see you tomorrow."

Lester Lange looked like he'd lost the weight of the proverbial albatross as he picked up his hat and jauntily plopped it onto his head, jogged down the steps, and went on his merry way.

She watched him go. Now what? Running into him like this had kicked her neat little world on its butt. One gnawing question had been answered: she knew why he'd jumped ship so long ago. But knowing that had summoned up a new question, one that loomed over her like a tempest sweeping in from a stormy sky.

She didn't know yet exactly what she would do, but she did know she had a lot to do before noon the next day, much more than whipping up lunch. It was late; she'd wait until morning to get started, she decided.

Looking skyward, she prayed, "Dear Lord, help me make it through the day tomorrow. It's going to be a humdinger!"

Chapter 16

Leah gaped, unable to comprehend what she was seeing; it was so unexpected. "Grady! Gracie!" She popped out of her rocking chair, flew down the porch steps, flung open the gate, and fell into her children's arms.

"Cassie, come, meet my family." Leah motioned for her new bestie to join them. She made introductions all the way around, elated to have her children with her.

"We couldn't let your birthday go by without coming to celebrate with you," her daughter said.

"Everybody else'll be here this weekend, but don't worry. We're staying at the B&B two doors down. We know this place is too small, and it's your painting studio." Her son alluded to his wife, Gracie's husband, the grandchildren, and the great-grandchild.

"Wait! It's your birthday? You didn't tell me." Cassie shook a finger at Leah.

"She never tells anybody," Gracie said. "She likes to keep it a secret, but we won't let her get away with that. It's tomorrow. Sixty-five years old and looking fantastic."

"Oh-h-h." Leah hugged her daughter again. "You're the beautiful one in this family, with those Italian good looks you got from your father." She ran a palm along the side of her daughter's luxuriant black hair. "I'm so glad you're here." She turned to her son. "Grady, I've been trying to call and text you all morning. We need to talk. I've been quite frantic about it. It's important."

"That's true. I've never seen her on her phone like that," Cassie said. "I even helped her get lunch ready because she's been trying so hard to reach you, although she refuses to tell me why. But any time somebody asks me to help cook, that's a sign it's serious, and they have no other option left on earth." She didn't sound serious at all, however, as she teased her friend.

Grady cocked his head, looking at his mom inquisitively. "Okay, Mom. I guess I forgot to turn my phone on this morning." He took it out of his pocket, glanced at it, and put it away, not worried about that now. "Let's talk. But first, I've got to hit the little boy's room." He hoisted up his backpack, grabbed his sister's roller bag, and headed for the cottage.

"Wait! I'm coming with you..." Leah trailed her son inside.

"Oh lordy," Gracie said with a chuckle as she and Cassie sidled up the walk. "She's going to knock on the bathroom door and talk to him through the wood like she did when we were kids."

"Hello."

The women turned around to be greeted by an attractive man standing at the gate.

"Lester! Come in. This is Leah's daughter, Gracie. Her kids came to surprise her for her birthday tomorrow."

Lester came through the gate. "Hi, Cassie. Hello, Gracie. It's so very nice to meet you. I had no idea it was your mother's birthday."

Cassie didn't say a word as she watched Gracie pale at the sight of Lester, a man she'd only just met. Cassie didn't know what that meant, but she did know that something was going on here that she knew absolutely nothing about. What was it that she was missing? It felt like it was right in front of her....

Finally, Gracie stirred. "Hello, Lester. Let me get my mom." Leah's daughter fled into the cottage as if trying to escape a phantom.

The other two followed her disappearance with their gaze and stared at the door of the cottage as if a miracle might materialize from within. It did. Leah and Grady, with Gracie in their wake, bounded out the door and stood like specters on a stage.

Lester's heart skipped a beat. Then, in one swoop, he miraculously felt stronger than he'd felt in years, joy invigorating every fiber of his being – his bones, his muscles, his soul all suddenly feeling whole. He walked up to the bottom of the steps and looked up at Leah's son.

He was looking at himself, only younger.

"Hello, Lester. I'm Grady." The younger man came down the steps and shook hands with the man who so obviously was his father.

Chapter 17

C assie now knew for certain what she would write about for her article on Mackinac Island. She jotted down the title on her notepad:

Magical Mackinac Island: The Healing Power of Stepping Back in Time

She realized she'd witnessed that firsthand only hours before.

Thinking it best to leave Leah's family alone to sort out their lives together, she left them and came to one of her favorite spots on the island, a rocking chair on the back porch of the library. The rhythm of the waves lapping against the shore served as a metronome, inspiring the words of her story to flow onto the page...

From the moment you step onto the island, you step back in time not only historically but personally, as well. You're transported to a time in your life when you felt whole and hopeful and happy, a time when the worries of the world faded away, at least for a little while. You see yourself from a distance, gaining perspective on your daily life. You rest and reflect, which enables you to absorb the healing power of this magical place and become mindful of a purposefulness that may have been lost in the chaos of living.

You might simply want to sit a spell and sip lemonade or stand by the lake remembering to breathe. Or you might want to delve more deeply into your life and consider how you live and whether that makes you happy. In any of those instances, you will renew your faith in yourself and your ability to live the life that is right for you....

There was another reason she knew about the magic of the island. It had happened to her. Totally unexpected, it gobsmacked her into scrutinizing her life. Her carefully constructed existence in New York City now seemed like a movie of someone else's robotic daily routine, unrecognizable as anything that related to her. She could sit back and objectively see the images on the screen in her mind, watching as the initial excitement of city living swept her away without thought.

Moving in with her boyfriend had solidified her absorption into a way of thinking that became almost cultish, as if she'd handed over her own brain to the other members. She and her boyfriend repeatedly met up with friends at the same trendy bars for happy hour. They moved from the bar to a flashy restaurant almost every night of the week, feeling like bigshots, posing for the same crowd over and over again. Sleek, sophisticated, hot.

And broke. At least for her. The truth was that once she moved out of her jerk of a boyfriend's apartment, she couldn't afford city living. She'd been bored by it all, anyway. She'd lived with the man for two years, but not once until now had he crossed her mind since the second day she'd been here. And she wasn't advancing in her career for reasons she needed to ascertain. And she wasn't happy.

She'd been jotting down the list as the thoughts came to her. It was quite a list.

The evening before, after she'd confessed that she hated her usually thankless job and that she didn't make enough money to support her life in the city, Russ had asked her if there was any chance she could remain on the island for the rest of the summer. He offered to have her stay at the house with him and Miranda and to put her to work with the horses, which she'd discovered she loved. Another shocker. She'd never even had a cat.

She'd declined the offer for the whole summer, seeing that her next job assignment was already lined up – a resort in the Adirondacks in upstate New York in a week. She might not like her boss, but she wouldn't leave her in the lurch, quitting without appropriate notice. She decided to hand in her two-week resignation, finish that assignment, and then come back to the island. That would give her the rest of the summer to explore what to do with her journalism career. She didn't want to give it up entirely, but she needed to take it in another direction. The prospect terrified and excited her at the same time. If she had to go back to waitressing in the fall, she knew from five years of doing that while in college that she was good at it. It could get her by temporarily if need be.

As for her apartment in the city, she had ten months left on her lease. She'd be able to sublet it in a nano second in that bustling metropolis. She'd go back, move out, store her stuff, do the Adirondacks, and return to Mackinac Island. By fall, she'd have to figure out a whole new life. Her head spun at the thought. She put all that aside and went back to writing her article.

"There you are, good lookin'. I thought I'd find you here." Russ appeared on the library porch, interrupting her thoughts. It felt like a ray of sunshine had entered her sphere. He bent down to kiss her, soft and warm, leaving her wanting more of those kisses for a long time to come.

He sat beside her, and she told him the incredible story of Leah and Lester and of their child.

When she finished, he said, "That's amazing. Good things do show up in our lives, don't they?"

"Yes. Yes, they do. The trick is to recognize them when they're right in front of you."

He playfully spread out his arms in a display of "here I am."

Cassie Evans hadn't been this happy in a very long time. She had no idea where all of this was headed, but she knew she couldn't go back to what had been.

Chapter 18

"I met Frank when I was six months pregnant. The truth is, I was so devastated and despondent when I never heard from you that I was practically insane with confusion. My parents wanted me to give the baby up for adoption. I couldn't do it. I wanted my baby. They were furious with me. Then Frank came along and accepted me as I was: huge with someone else's child, depressed, and helpless. He coaxed me out of my sorry state and gave me the support I so desperately needed. His parents were so kind and gentle with me. To them, another baby in the world was a miracle. That whole family made me feel like maybe I wasn't the most stupid, worthless girl alive. Frank and I married a week before Grady was born."

Leah took a break and sipped on her glass of wine. Her kids had left her and Lester to talk things out after father and son had agreed to meet later for supper. The former lovers sat on her porch, each with a glass of wine at hand.

Lester started to speak, but she put up a hand to stop him. "I need for you to know that Frank was a wonderful father. Grady and Gracie adored him, and I wouldn't want it any other way. He raised Grady like his own son, never giving one iota of a hint that he thought of him in any other way. Frank never missed a school event or game

87

or anything either of the kids were doing. He tossed a ball a thousand times when Grady was practicing for baseball and football. The two of them putzed around in the garage, working on old junker cars. They loved that. I'd hear them out there laughing and teasing each other. More recently, they played golf together all the time, Grady's treat. I never heard Frank say so much as a cross word to either child." She shook her head. "In fact, if any punishment was ever called for, I was the one who had to do it because Frank was far too soft-hearted to scold anybody." A whimsical grin crossed her lips. "He was a good man."

Lester let her words seep in, pleased with himself that they didn't conjure up feelings of jealousy or remorse. It turned out he was a bigger man than he'd suspected. "Rose, I think I would've liked Frank."

She nodded. "Oh, you would have. Everybody did. When Grady was eighteen, we told him about you. It seemed the fair thing to do. We told Gracie, too, when she was old enough. Frank even offered to help Grady find you if he wanted to. He was so sure of his son's love, he didn't feel threatened by that at all. But Grady didn't want to. I know it was because he didn't want to slight his dad in any way. Since Frank's death, though, Grady's been asking me about you, and I know he's been thinking of trying to find you. And here you are. I still can't quite believe it."

"Me, either. Thank you."

"For what?"

"For raising our son so well. For giving him a stable home and a good father. Thank you." He ran a finger along the brim of his hat on the table, as if that helped him gather courage. "Rose, do you think... Well, do you think you and I might spend more time together and see if we still like each other?"

Leah pondered that as she took a drink.

"I think I need to think things over, Lester," she finally admitted. She fussed with her wedding ring, twisting it around. "I need to paint for a while. That always helps me think. It's been a momentous afternoon."

"Of course. I'll take my leave and hope to see you later. Call me if you need anything. Any time. I'll be happy to do anything I can for you."

He got up and started to go but hesitated. "Rose, you loved Frank, didn't you? He was the love of your life, wasn't he?"

The question caught her off guard. She took a breath, and her voice caught in her throat as she rasped, "Yes."

Having known that was going to be her answer, Lester nodded his understanding and steadfastly shored himself up to walk home.

Chapter 19

Lester strolled his backyard, biding his time until Grady – his son! – would arrive in half an hour. He might plant an apple tree there, he thought as he examined a rather empty spot by the side fence, and he could install a flagstone pathway from the deck to the back gate. Pausing at the gate, his arms folded on top of it, he surveyed the lake, at the moment, as smooth as a sheet of aqua-blue silk.

It calmed him.

The front doorbell rang, its chime echoing all the way through the house. It surprised him; it was too early for Grady.

When he opened the door, "surprise" didn't cover it.

"Hi." Leah – Rose to him – stood there. "May I come in?"

"Of course."

He ushered her in, and she immediately scanned the living room, touching here and there, remembering the place from so long ago.

Lester put his hands in his pockets and waited.

"All these years," she finally said, "and the few times I came back to the island, I was afraid to look at this cottage when I rode by. I didn't want to wonder about you. I was afraid it would bring back too many memories and hurt too much."

She wandered outside and meandered to the gate to take in Lake Huron, the same scene Lester had been enjoying.

"Lester."

"Yes."

She faced him. "Frank was the love of my life. He was there for me for most of my life."

Lester's hopes plummeted. He was a doomed man.

"But you, Lester, are the love of my dreams. I'd like very much for us to spend time together to see if dreams can come true."

Lester's heart took a joyous leap. As he stepped closer to her, he noticed that her wedding ring had been replaced by his grandmother's ring, the one he gave her when he asked her to marry him. Gently, he took her hand and fingered the ring. Then he drew her to him. The kiss was long and sweet.

This time, he promised himself, he'd never let her go.

Leah Rose stood alone on the shore, a light breeze sweeping wisps of hair about her face. She savored the rather bohemian sensation of feeling free to let nature do as it wished. She'd stood in this very spot when she was eighteen years old, back then feeling as if the whole world, full of promise and possibility, lay before her. Forty-seven years later, to her utter amazement, she felt the same way.

As it turned out, she'd discovered that hopeful young woman, staggering as the awareness had been, still living within her. The young one had been buried under the debris of an overworked, busy life for far too long and had arisen to insist on reclaiming her place within this sixty-five-year-old body.

"I will never bury you away again," Leah vowed to her younger self. "I will cherish you and protect you, allowing nothing but goodness to come our way. I will be happy again."

With that, she hopped onto her bicycle and rode back to her cottage, where she plucked a lilac and put it in her hair.

* * *

Author's Note: I hope you enjoyed reading this story as much as I enjoyed writing it. Mackinac Island is one of my favorite places on earth. I've been visiting there since I was a kid.

Your reviews mean the world to me. To leave one for this novella please click here:

https://www.amazon.com/review/create-review?&asin= B093RZSF9Z

You may have noticed that I didn't give specific names for lodgings (except the iconic Grand Hotel), restaurants, or shops (except for the fudge shops). That is because I didn't want to connote that any are better than others. I've stayed in many inns and B&Bs and have eaten everywhere. It's all good!

If you've never been to the island, I hope this story imbued you with its ambiance, history, and friendliness. We too seldom experience places like that anymore. Ride a bike. Take a carriage ride. Maybe even ride a horse. And, for goodness' sake, eat fudge.

As Cassie wrote, it's the kind of place where "...you will renew your faith in yourself and your ability to live the life that is right for you...."

Here's my first trip to Mackinac Island at age nine, with my dad and little sister. (Mom took the picture.)

More in the "Shades of Hope" Collection:

Each novella in my Shades of Hope collection stands alone, with different characters and settings. However, they all offer second chance romances, endearing friendships, and a promise of hope.

Next up is *Gold Mountain:*

There might be gold in them that hills, but San Francisco tycoon Caden Caldwell heads for Alaska in a fit of rage looking for his free-spirited son, Colt, who has struck out for adventure in the Klondike Gold Rush in 1896. What Caden finds is something else altogether. Orphaned children. Wayward women. Quirky prospectors. Tlingit Indians.

Isolated with this bunch when winter weather hits, he has no choice but to re-evaluate his life. Will he ever be the same? Does he want to be? The highfalutin mogul just might be brought down to earth to strike it rich in ways he never imagined.

Order it here: My Book - *Gold Mountain* on Amazon

amazon.com/Gold-Mountain-Shades-Novella-Collection-ebook/dp/B08R2D6SNP

Here are the first two chapters:

Chapter 1

Colt Caldwell bolted over the white picket fence and sprinted as fast as his aroused physical condition would allow. A second bullet shot past his head, missing by a mere few inches, even closer than the first one.

"Damn!" He yelped, ducking like a scared cat. He begged his already strained limbs to work harder and faster.

"You son-of-a-bitch! Stay away from my wife!" The gruff voice twenty yards behind him could be heard all over their posh Nob Hill neighborhood in San Francisco. Another shot careened off a tree, this one missing its mark by a bunch.

The old guy was getting tired and careless, Colt calculated. "Thank you, Jesus," he rasped as he continued to sprint through another backyard like ... well, like a rake caught naked with another man's wife. Another fence, another leap, and suddenly good fortune loomed ahead. Lilac bushes, thick and tall. He blasted through them, immersed in their pleasant pungent scent for the short moments it took him to spring to the other side.

An old woman stood at a clothesline, casually gathering laundry and folding it neatly into a large basket that sat at her feet. She had looked in the direction of the confusing commotion that she couldn't see through her patch of foliage. When the buck naked young man burst through her flower bushes, with a scattering of dainty lilac petals entangled in his thick black hair, she wasn't shocked, for some reason she would never have been able to explain. Instead of being surprised or afraid, she simply watched with interest as the lanky, muscled specimen flew past her.

"Oh, so sorry, ma'am," he managed as he went by.

"Here." She tossed him a large towel.

An enormous grin erupted across his square-jawed face as he secured the towel around his waist. Refusing to be rude to a woman, even if it meant his life, he jaunted sideways and bussed her on her aged cheek. "Thank you, love," he called back as he disappeared around the side of her house.

Her mouth edged upward as a smile whittled its way onto her face. Rivulets of wrinkles turned into tributaries that flowed across her skin as her delight eddied like none had in a long time.

She hadn't seen an erection like that since .... hmmm. Never, she decided. At least, not like *that*.

Spinning on her heels in response to noise behind her, she watched as a corpulent, gasping, middle-aged man stumbled around the side of her lilac bushes. She recognized him as her neighbor from three doors down but couldn't recall his name. He'd never impressed her enough to make the effort.

"Have you ..." He stopped to bend over, hands on his knees, gulping in deep breaths. A pistol dangled from a finger of one hand. "Have you ..." He breathed so raggedly she hoped he wouldn't conk out from an apoplectic fit right there in her garden. That would be so messy. "Have you seen a naked young man?" He finally got it out.

"Why, no, sir. I am certain I would have noticed such a thing."

"Damn it all to hell. He must have dodged in-between the houses back there." He pointed in the direction he'd come from and turned to go. "I'll catch that bastard yet," the cuckold groused as he left.

The old woman turned to peer at the spot where the naked young man had disappeared. She stroked her cheek where he'd kissed her.

This was the best day she'd had in years.

Chapter 2

Colt O'Connor Caldwell! Get down here!" Caden Caldwell's furious baritone bounced off the walls of his cavernous foyer. A freight train may as well have been barreling through the opulent room. Hand gripping the ornate newel post, he glared up the wide staircase and bellowed again. "Colt! I said get your sorry ass down here!"

"He's gone."

The fifty-two-year-old tycoon jerked around to confront the source of the stern statement. His housekeeper, Miss Farmington, fussed with a feathery bonnet she held. Nonplussed despite her employer's tantrum, she pulled a pearl-tipped hatpin out of the side of the hat and went to the hall tree to look in the mirror. She put the hat on so as not to disturb her neat chignon, making certain the feathers were cocked just so, then stuck the pin through the fabric and a clump of hair to keep her millinery in place.

"Where is he?" The words spewed out in a growl with Caden's jaw clenched so tightly his trimmed mustache didn't bother to move. "The livery driver told me he was running through the neighborhood wearing nothing more than a towel. No doubt having been caught again bedding another innocent young woman."

"Not so innocent. This one was married. He said to tell you he's sorry if the woman's husband pays you an unpleasant visit."

"Damn it! Where is he?" The tall man's neck and face reddened inch-by-inch, like mercury rising in a thermometer in the heat of an angry fever. "If you're hiding him—"

"I told you, he's gone," she interrupted. "For good this time." Now she picked up a pair of white lace gloves from a side table and put them on, methodically stretching each finger, as if mocking him.

Suddenly it struck him that she was going somewhere. There were three travel bags stacked by the door, and she wore a summery traveling suit in a pale green that complimented her blue-green eyes. Thank the moon and stars, he thought, that she no longer wore one of those bustley things that had been so popular with women for many years but had recently gone out of style. He never had understood why females wanted to stick a basket over their derrières to make them look bigger. At the moment, Miss Farmington looked downright fetching, especially for a woman who must be nigh on forty-five years old.

He swept the uninvited thought from his mind. Why on earth would he ever think about a housekeeper as being attractive?

"Where are you going?"

"I told you last week that when Colt finally left for good, I would quit. He's the only reason I've stayed in the employment of a scoundrel like you for all these years. He's gone, and so am I.

"I've summoned a carriage. A porter will pick up my bags this afternoon. Good-bye, Mr. Caldwell." She picked up a parasol and sauntered to the door. Her hand reached for the knob.

"Wait! What in blazes? You can't quit and leave me in the lurch. Why, that's totally unethical."

Miss Farmington's hand froze over the rubbed bronze doorknob as her mind churned with retorts. Her disdain for him was so obvious he could almost see it prancing around inside her head. Then, instantly, as if a herd of wild horses had broken loose from their corral, she turned to her now former employer with such a leer that he stepped back in alarm at the impending stampede.

With the grace and speed of a thoroughbred, the woman came at him, parasol raised in fury. Totally befuddled, Caden scuttled further back, bumped into the newel post, and skidded sideways to take cover behind a high-back chair.

She shook the umbrella up and down in his direction. "I'm unethical? Me?" He'd never heard this screeching tone of voice from her in the entire twenty-one years she'd been in his employ. It was as if a belligerent barmaid had possessed his proficient housekeeper's body.

"Let me tell you, Mr. Smart-ass, about unethical."

Caden blinked and sputtered in shock at the verbal attack as she pointed the tip of her menacing weapon right at his face. He flung his head back as far as possible.

"Unethical was when Colt was a baby and you hired me to be his nanny after your wife died. God bless her sweet soul for ever putting up with a tyrant like you. Do you remember what you said to me my very first day on the job? Huh? Do you remember?"

He shook his head, dodging side to side, avoiding the stabbing stick as best he could.

"Well, I remember good and well. You told me to do whatever I wanted with him, because you didn't have time for a baby. Your own son." Her voice seethed with disgust. "I told you right then and there that without a mother the child needed a father more than ever. But no-o-o. You were too busy with your damned businesses.

"I gave you leeway because I figured your wife had recently died and you'd come to your senses in time. Well, it's been twenty-one years and you haven't yet. How many times over all these years have I told you that your son needed you? How many times?"

He shook his head again and added a helpless shrug.

She lowered her makeshift weapon and her voice softened, infused with sorrow now as well as anger. "I've done my best over the years. I love that young man as if he were my own child. Praise be to God, I'm the closest thing to a mother he's ever had. Do you honestly think that once he no longer needed a nanny I stayed on as your housekeeper for the pleasure of it? No! I stayed for Colt, but that boy has needed a father all of his life."

Caden became struck by the tears that pooled in her eyes, recalling that this scene had played out a number of times over the years, although always with more proper decorum. He'd routinely dismissed her as a silly nuisance. Now he suspected that maybe he should have paid more attention.

"In case you never noticed," she went on, leaning on the umbrella like a cane, "he is a wonderful young man. Not like you. Yes, he likes the girls too much. He's needed a father to talk to him about that rather than yell at him about it. But he is also brilliant and creative and kindhearted and charming and full of adventure. So much adventure!" A whimsical grin crossed her lips.

"I know. I know." Caden put up his palms in defense. "I do know my son, despite what you think. I know he has some good qualities, things that will serve him well when I bring him into the business—"

"He doesn't want to be in your damned property development business!" She pounded the tip of the umbrella on the marble floor three times. "He's told you that a hundred times. He has his own dreams. His own desires." A tear rolled down her cheek. She swiped it away with dramatic flair. "And now he's gone. He kissed me on the cheek, told me he loves me, and promised to write to me. From Juneau. He's joining the Alaska gold rush. He said he needs some adventure. And then he walked right out that door." She jabbed a finger at the front door.

"Good-bye, Mr. Caldwell." Straightening her spine in a show of defiance, Miss Farmington walked out.

"Wait!"

Caden's clarion call was drowned out by the slam of the front door. He moved out from behind the chair and stood in the middle of his grand foyer, stunned. People simply did not walk out on Caden Caldwell. Sure, his butler had quit the day before, but certainly he would return. That was it. No matter what that rude housekeeper thought, Caden knew without a doubt that his son would return, too. After all, how could that wild young colt possibly make it on his own? As for Miss Farmington, when she came back, stupid feathery hat in hand, he'd have to deny her return.

"What impudence, talking to me like that." Mustering up his usual sense of mastery over his wedge of the world, he pulled down on the lapels of his coal black, immaculately tailored suit coat as if that secured his bluster. Mollified, for the moment at least, he went into his study and closed the door.

A teenaged maid; dressed in the manor's traditional starched blue uniform, white apron, and white hat, with feather duster in hand; peeked out into the foyer from behind the parlor door. Trepidatious, she looked in all directions. Finding the room void of its master, she scurried into the back of the house. Five minutes later she appeared again, uniform apron and hat having disappeared, a tattered straw hat on her head. With the adeptness of a thieving picklock, she opened the front door, slipped outside, and closed the door behind her. Two weeks, she'd decided, of being the downstairs maid under the same roof with that Mister Caden Caldwell had been enough to last her a lifetime.

About the Author

Linda Hughes is an Amazon #1 bestselling co-author and award-winning author. A world traveler and native Michigander, she lives in Oklahoma with her husband Joe, two dogs, and a cat. She visits Mackinac Island every summer.

More Shades of Hope novellas:

Black Forest
Gold Mountain
Green Valley (coming in 2023)
Blue Ice (coming in 2023)

More novels by Linda Hughes:

Becoming Jessie Belle: Book 1 (Indie Book of the Day)
Becoming Jessie Belle: Book 2
Becoming Jessie Belle: Book 3
Secrets of the Asylum (eLit Bronze and Silver Falchion finalist)
Secrets of the Island (Baltic Writing Award finalist)
Secrets of the Summer (Murder and Mayhem Award finalist)
The Burly-Q Girls: The 6
The Burly-Q Girls: 6 Dicks
The Burly-Q Girls: 6' Under
The House on Haven Island
Tough Rocks

Find Linda at:

Website – www.lindahughes.com (sign up for her newsletter for a free copy of *The House on Haven Island,* and for updates and special offers.)

Amazon author's page – Linda Hughes

Facebook – /lindahughesauthor

Instagram – @lghughesauthor

YouTube – Linda Hughes, Author

www.ingramcontent.com/pod-product-compliance
Lightning Source LLC
Chambersburg PA
CBHW070336120726
47909CB00008B/2703

* 9 7 8 0 5 7 8 9 7 0 2 6 4 *